I0746558

The Sun Shines a Little Brighter Today

The Sun Shines a Little Brighter Today

ANDRES H. CORTES

To my mom.

To God.

Lo que el escritor inventa primero es el personaje que escribirá sus obras.

— Nicolás Gómez Dávila, Escolios a un texto implícito.

I

It's a sunny afternoon. Some golden rays filter through the branches of the bare trees, poised on the threshold of winter, entering through my window and gently caressing my skin. My withered skin. It's neither cold nor hot; the whole room feels warm, almost like...

As I sip some water on this peculiar day, the yellow hues of the light—foretelling the arrival of the dark azure night—remind me of Victor, a person I never met but whose presence lingers like an echo. The orange tones cast a final glow of life on my pale hands, resting on the keyboard, about to open a portal. In this moment, I can feel the rhythmic weight of his fingers on the keys of a different computer, imprinting letters on a white background, forming waves that reverberate through my mind, oscillations of light interrupted only by his relentless shadow.

I came to know him through a text he wrote—one I read exactly twenty years ago, tucked away on a USB drive I found in a room

I had just rented. My age: twenty-one; he, at the beginning of the text, was thirty-three.

Back then, I tried to understand him, but I was sceptical. His words and contradictions, like strokes on a canvas, created colours, tones, and shapes in a world I had never known. Time lent weight to his strange brushstrokes, magnified his mistakes, and through his filters, I glimpsed a reality. Now that I am older, I've come to believe I never truly understood him. I wish I could say otherwise.

I see myself the first time I read it—sitting at the computer, the blurred reflection of my young face in the grimy window beside me, my long hair falling across my shoulders, my blue eyes winking back at me in time. The text began abruptly, as if I'd opened a private diary at random. There was no introduction, no context—just a date and these raw, unfiltered thoughts from someone I didn't know, about a woman and a day in February. Today, for reasons I can't entirely explain, I begin to read it again.

"Friday, 30 August

In my mind, the purple night is embedded—a moment when my body swam through my room's darkness, weightless yet heavy. I sank into the chair and switched on my computer, but the dim light from the screen was swallowed by shadows. I reached for the lamp to my right—my steadfast companion these past two years—and flicked it on. Its glow spilled across my fingers, revealing the worn letters on the keys. Outside, the drizzle tapped against the window, echoing the soft rhythm of my fingertips on the keyboard. I felt as though the rain remembered the tears that once blurred my solitary nights.

It was one of those countless evenings when inspiration struck, yet this one stands apart from all the others. On that occasion, I resolved to write about myself—as I am doing now, and as I will keep doing until I discover an ending. A worthy one.

That night carried an extra weight; my mind, my heart, my psyche, my soul—whatever it was—was in pain because my ex-girlfriend at the time, how peculiar that she was already my ex, had told me through a text message that it was better if we didn't see each other anymore. Reading her words hurled me into a black hole. I said nothing—I didn't reply. Recalling our brightest moments now feels so *sad*. I loved that woman deeply—perhaps I frame it in the past tense, though honesty insists it belongs in the present.

It would be dazzling—almost a decadent pleasure—to believe that purple dusk belongs to a distant past.

But it doesn't.

Tonight—the darkness that still grazes my skin as I write—her message was received just minutes ago. The wound is still bleeding.

I will always remember that sunny February day when I met her, a day when I couldn't stop feeling as though life was slipping through my fingers, even as my hands were busy drying dishes. I tried to appear energetic in the eyes of my supervisor so she'd think I was motivated, that I liked my job, that I embraced the identity this work imposed on me—so different from the one I felt should be mine.

My eyes—windows to my soul—watched people come and go. Had anyone looked closely, they would have seen the reflection of that inner weariness: the ache of becoming what you must, instead of who you truly want to be. Minutes I wished I could use for anything else would have felt more eternal. But in that moment, I felt the weight of the world—enough to painfully remind me that I was alive. That discomfort was necessary to awaken my mind and make my soul beat. Thousands of ideas attacked me; my thoughts blossomed. Out of the misery I saw in this activity, something within me elevated it, almost beautified it, even romanticised it. It became something necessary— as if even the most trivial things, for someone who knows how to describe them, could be touched by the light of the sublime. And the shadow that forms from this is the filth one has to live with. What a fucking shit it was to find inspiration in such moments—but that, too, was an act of rebellion. My labour was worth a few dollars an hour, but my mind did not work for them. I was aware of what was happening: conversations with myself that made me feel rotten, but ones I wouldn't trade for an instant, because they made me who I was, who I still am, how I thought, how I think. If I were different, that version of me would have been more complacent, and I wouldn't have written this.

That same sunny day in February, while the hot water licked my hands and the soap's foam slowly swallowed more of my arms, she walked into my workplace—a place that sold "fast food", which isn't even worth mentioning. There I was, a 33-year-old dishwasher who also manned the register whenever needed—the foreigner trying to make a living in the First World. She stood in front of the counter, accompanied by someone I didn't even bother to notice. My job wasn't to notice; it was to serve, to deliver what the customer ordered, and return to my daydreams at the sink. Her companion ordered the trashiest item on the menu—fried chicken drenched in oil—something I wouldn't eat even by accident—while she ordered something from the vegan menu.

The interaction unfolded like a music video: the dazzling young woman locking eyes with the handsome 'worker' (in quotes, of course). The spark of intrigue was lit, the intensity of the melody set the scene, and the singer's voice entered with the first verse. Obviously, the scene was in black-and-white, but when she moved her exquisite lips, they turned red, and suddenly, colour flooded this corner of the universe like rays of light breaking through a pale, absent afternoon rain, forming a rainbow. Her big brown eyes met my green ones, and for a second, I thought I saw the reflection of my eyelashes dancing on her white teeth. Then I noticed a tiny mark on her chin. The tips of her hair teasingly and shamelessly caressed her ass, and the nonexistent cameraman focused on her from behind to capture a sweeping view of her beautiful figure.

"I like your tattoos," she said, her voice soft, unbothered, slightly husky—a voice that travelled the metre between us and effortlessly split my life in two.

She knew it.

I knew it.

Destiny knew it.

I replied, "Thank you."

She smiled, turned away, and the moment was sealed. The stars applauded, the moon—absent yet aware—sighed as the sun whispered into her ear what had just happened.

The rest of that shift was dedicated to thinking about her. Again and again, the grey matter in my skull replayed the scene from different angles. I watched myself, imagined how she saw me, perceived me, smelt me... I even detested myself for not having said something more. I filled the absence of wit in that moment with an overabundance of imagination, opening different doors with alternate responses, all of which led to her thinking about me.

After that day, my mind relaxed a little, but at the most inopportune and unexpected moments, the scene would arise again, uncalled for. Her words to me kept my loneliness company: "I like your tattoos." They stirred the yellow butterflies swirling around me, subtly hinting at where I came from—those fluttering yellow wings betraying more than just my origin.

I had been living in this cold corner of the world for a year and three months. Why was I here? Just a strategy to get a document that would let me stay in the First World without torturing myself with the thought of returning to my country. A year and three months in which I hadn't made a single friend. My theory was that I was too old to make friends, lacking the patience to plaster on a smile and try to understand someone else's soul. Perhaps it was a reflection of many fears and that wretched urge to romanticise Solitude—that Solitude that is a bad counsellor, that pushes but doesn't let go, the kind that never leaves because it feeds on our very existence. If you embrace it, it shows you who you are, but it's also a trap because knowing you're a lonely person is one thing, but being one is another. Adapting to the role demands sacrifices that deform the psyche."

I have read this text countless times, and I always pause at the word "psyche", just as I did the first time, on the evening of a distant December in that "corner of the world". A pause followed by a grimace—my lips stretching as if for an anxious kiss, I remember thinking, "What an overdramatic and solitary man," my incredulous eyes rolling slightly to the right, uninterested. That grimace never returned in all the times I've revisited the opening paragraphs.

I can see myself on that second night in that desolate room. I was half-naked, with a bed covered by a single sheet, a mini-fridge holding a dozen eggs I'd bought earlier that afternoon, a chair with a white desk and my computer resting on it, two unpacked suitcases, and an old three-bulb chandelier with only one working light. Together, they lent my youth an air of independence.

Independence that I believed I had earned through a lie. It had been almost three years since I finished school. I was never known for being a good or bad student, and I didn't know what I wanted from myself—or from life—at that time. My mother's silence on the matter was either the trust I believed she had in me, or the knowledge she already possessed—that it wasn't worth adding any weight to my already light existence. Her attention had shifted to another man, someone who was neither my father nor me, leaving me with a growing sense of invisibility, which I liked. I could not blame her. My father, on the other hand, was a distant figure, almost blurry and absent on many occasions. He was like the warmth of a far-off sun in the middle of winter—promising to return on cold mornings, bright but powerless, leaving us at the mercy of warm clothing that would make us less dependent on him. Occasionally, he would interfere in my life, demanding something of me that he had never cultivated in me or even himself. Perhaps he did this out of love, or perhaps because he wanted to rid himself of a responsibility he had never fully embraced. For that very reason, I tried to avoid conversations about my future whenever we crossed paths. His stance was always a point-blank barrage of suggestions, delivered with varying tones of concern and veiled threats about what awaited me if I didn't follow his advice. The problem was that his effervescence fizzled out as soon as our infrequent encounters ended.

There was never any follow-up. I think he had memorised the lines he repeated, the grimaces, the moment he would glance at his phone to announce it was time to leave, and his "I love you", which, to this day, I still believe was the only genuine thing. His grand performance the first time had quite literally made me believe in his interest. Over time, I too learned to respond with gestures, excuses, and promises. There was no doubt—I was my father's son. The narrowing and expansion of shadows in my room symbolise the afternoon losing its strength, reaching the threshold of its magnificence. The ease with which the night falls slowly pulls me away from my memories for a moment. I glance at the glass of water, begging to be refilled, while the screen's light draws my attention again. Hunger gnaws at my stomach, but laziness keeps me in place—or perhaps it doesn't, but I'd rather just go to the window, hoping to see the sanguine dawn piercing through the houses and trees that obstruct the horizon. I imagine that once darkness floods my surroundings, I'll take two steps, raise my hand to shoulder height, and with my index finger, press a click that will drain the night. Then, I'll return to my desk to reread the text—though perhaps it's a better idea to get more water. Maybe I'll grab something to eat while I'm at it. I return to my room after going to the bathroom, something that wasn't part of my plans but felt necessary. I didn't want to leave my room again for the rest of the night unless it was to brush my teeth and go straight to bed. For that reason, I carried a full pitcher of water in my hand. Slowly, I sit down in front of the desk. I glance out the window, and there aren't many lights on in the surrounding houses—it seems like a mirror of the starless night that blankets our rest. I feel melancholically at ease.

The empty glass pleads for help, and I watch as my right hand lifts the pitcher, tilting it to pour water into the glass, filling it little by little. When it reaches the brim, I lift my gaze and see my father before me, watching me fill a different glass more than twenty years ago. There he was, launching into his usual histrionic display, repeating his speech full of warnings and advice that had long since turned into noise. I blink, trying to put on my interested face, making gestures to encourage him to go on. I blink again and find myself back in my room, though I remember that moment so vividly—as if I were an observer watching the interaction between my father and me. I can see how I gathered the courage to act counterintuitively, to step out of the role I was meant to play. I watch myself take a deep breath, my face full of vigour, slightly tanned and somewhat feminine, with no trace of experience. My father looks at me intently, waiting for the same monologue full of excuses to come from my mouth. But not that day. That day, instead of escaping, I wrapped myself in his mantle of protection. It was a turning point in our relationship. I told him I was going to study in another city, to build a future, and that

I obviously needed his financial help—to "lend me the money I needed". It caught him off guard. But the weight of his commitment to the persona he had crafted in front of me didn't let him escape. Even if he didn't want to, it made him more consistent with my idea, forcing him to accept and help me. I had given him a reason. He wasn't an idiot either. To this day, I believe he knew I was lying, but seeing that with a few extra dollars he could rid himself of a worn-out, moribund interaction, he protected us both. He could gain more freedom from me, and I from him. He agreed and lent me the money. Obviously, he asked many questions, and his body language was a wavering dance between certainty and uncertainty that fit perfectly into the interaction, giving it a sense of naturalness. For my part, I stayed silent and let him speak, agreeing with him and admitting that I should have listened to him earlier. It almost seemed as if we had both rehearsed for that moment. An unsummoned thought cuts through the images of my memory for a second, as if doubting whether what I imagined had truly happened, as if I, without realising it, had added or subtracted something from that moment—either assigning myself more guilt or feeling that it was justified. Time made me distrust the steps I had taken in the past, but my mind found ways to ensure that if I stumbled, the fall wouldn't be too harsh, at least for now. Occasionally after that, he would ask how everything was going, without much interest, and he never mentioned the money again. Our relationship became more like a friendship between two distant acquaintances.

23

A few years ago, I was in front of him again—not filling my glass this time, but his—at a hospital. He was lying on a stretcher, animatedly telling me about his life, while I knew he didn't have much time left in this world. But we both acted as if we didn't know. It was the pattern of our relationship.

I swallow, tasting the remnants of many tears that have wandered along the contours of my cheekbones when I think about this. "Enough, enough. Self-control," I tell myself, taking a sip of water and looking at the computer screen. I begin to read.

II

"The universe is riddled with mysteries we do not intend to find but cannot escape.

In the deepest corners of the cosmos, where our imagination reaches its peak, where irrationality clashes with nothingness—and perhaps nothingness itself is the horrifying answer—there lies a massive, large-scale flow of galaxy clusters moving uniformly at great speed. On a grand scale, it might seem like a slow, pre-ordained process. Like wild ants returning to the safety of their anthill after a vast undertaking of collection and exploration in their tiny ecosystem—or like weary labourers tracing the same tired paths back to their dwellings, only to rise again at dawn, slaves to a cycle they did not choose.

All this mass of cosmic matter is heading to a single point in space—I personally believe that we are also part of this same movement, but billions of light-years away, even though this damned gravitational force is beyond our observable universe. This phenomenon is so massive that experts call it a catastrophic event that began in the early days of our universe. Others say it's the point where our dimension separates from another. I say it's where God began everything, and whenever we finally reach that breach, that whirlpool that seems endless and absorbs everything, we will enter a cavity similar to a mouth, where gravitational forces act like molars, grinding the material and immaterial essence of what remains of us at that moment. The taste buds of this god will savour the sour and fetid flavour of hatred, envy, vengeance, and the countless atrocities committed not only by our humanity but by the innumerable races inhabiting the vast expanse of the universe.

At the moment it tastes the divine essence of love, salivary glands that emerge in my imagination will release intergalactic liquids, flooding every molecule in this cosmic bolus, giving destruction and transformation a purpose. This process will be eternal until even what lies beyond our vocabulary is stripped of all names. At that point, constrictor pharyngeal muscles, like black holes, will push us into an oesophagus where walls made of nebulae will perform peristaltic movements, transporting us in coordinated contractions to a stomach where light does not exist—the hell of nothingness, where everything is extinguished.

Our essence will decompose under corrosive acids that will strip away our dreams and sins. And this stomach will detect a problem; an interdimensional gastric irritation will arise—the reward or punishment for all our good and evil deeds will cause the diaphragm of this digestive system to contract, increasing pressure. The tension in time and space will collapse, and with a reverse peristaltic wave, it will hurl the contracted universe—condensed into a single mass—back through the mouth where everything ended… and began. Expelling us with an unprecedented force billions of light-years away—starting everything anew.

This threshold will close for a moment, only to once again draw back in everything it expelled, like that emaciated dog that consumes its own vomit, repeating this cosmic intoxication for all eternity. Absolutely everything will repeat again and again, including that "I like your tattoos" and, paradoxically, the fact that two days after this happened, I ran into her again as my co-worker.

I swear on everything sacred that I'm not lying. My eyes betrayed me and showed surprise; my face sought the best expression to hide the fear mixed with happiness of that moment. It was as if, in the middle of the desert, a thunderclap emerged from a cloudless sky and struck a dying tree, igniting a fire that didn't burn but conveyed an omen. How was it possible for this to happen? The universe is riddled with mysteries we do not intend to find but cannot escape… Although the answer was more than obvious: she had simply been applying for different jobs, and coincidence brought her to my side. I needed no further explanation. It was something destined to happen—a premonition, even though chance acted more on her behalf than mine. Her age—eighteen—led her to seek a job in her hometown where it was easy to find work. I knew her age because it was the first thing I asked her.

On the other hand, I had already lived in three different cities in different countries, jumping between various jobs that increasingly seemed incompatible with my age. But that's how mysterious life works—the universe's plan, destiny, or God's hand. Years and kilometres travelled so that my fantasy could get lost in those full lips I tried to avoid looking at. I knew from experience that she wasn't indifferent to me, and mysterious life, the universe's plan, destiny, or God's hand wasn't indifferent to me either.

She, of course, asked my age. From my lips came a poorly pronounced "33" with a thick Macondo-accent, though I could've easily said "25–29", and it would've been entirely believable—and much easier to pronounce. Not because I worked washing dishes but because time had treated me well, thanks to my parents' youthful genes and learning from past mistakes, avoiding turning them into habits. Besides, if this fucked-up system was gonna dangle the carrot of freedom and success, I figured I might as well play along. One day it was bound to throw me a bone, right? And when it did—when I finally got what I wanted—I wasn't gonna be caught dead with a soft belly and a broken back. Nah. I was gonna be sharp, lean, and ready to squeeze every drop of pleasure out of it.

That first day was fantastic; I wasn't present in the world. Despite my less-than-perfect command of English, our interaction flowed effortlessly. I teased her endlessly, pointing out how different we were and contradicting her at every turn. "We're enemies," I'd say with a grin, using my native Spanish to call her *enemiga*, and she, quick on her feet, would fire back, calling me *enemigo*. There was something playful in the way our words danced—a mischievous spark that made the language barrier seem like part of the game. My mind, while my hands were busy with water and soap, was fixed on her, imagining her stealing glances at me from the register—a cocky thought that overflowed with confidence and led me to get her Instagram, and, a few days later, confirm a date for Sunday of that same weekend at 3:13 p.m.

How beautiful it is to feel your heart beating with positive uncertainty. How pleasurable it is to walk, carrying a brain flooded with endorphins, euphoric over something that hasn't even happened—optimism. How good it felt to receive a message from her confirming that we'd meet. Illusion bloomed in the midst of my solitude— its blood-red petals recognising the sunlight, touched by the silver moon. Sounds of superstition at dawn foreshadowing the damp smell of dew on the coming Sunday. Seeing her brown eyes, knowing that in a few days they'd be fixed on me for longer, gave more meaning to everything I did—like every key I press at this moment, laden with nostalgia, resembling the steps I took in the past as I walked to our meeting point that Sunday.

I waited for her, sitting like a romantic vagabond pretending to be unbothered on a chair at the corner parallel to a bookstore. The sun asserted its dominance, leaving no clouds in the sky. At 3:14 p.m. her black skirt with red polka dots swayed, while her black boots stood out with confident, relaxed steps heading towards me. And her smile upon seeing me—a smile I hope repeats itself in the vastness of time and doesn't remain just letters produced by the weight of my solitude in this moment.

From her smile, I remember perfectly the unspoken hello. The scene was silent, like an eclipse; she interrupted the sun's rays striking my face diagonally. My eyes observed her intently, while my body and fears detached themselves from the chair until I managed to stand upright. I must confess, my mind played a cruel trick on me at that moment. How ironic—of all the vignettes which the most irrationally intimate and glorious scenarios had been sketched, only a single grey scene remained: her beautiful mouth carrying a polite smile.

That smile was a weapon disguised as courtesy, producing 12 lingual movements, beginning with her delicate tongue touching the upper part just behind her white front teeth to form the "T" sound, and ending with the final thrust as her tongue struck the roof of her mouth to release the "K." My eyes blinked in rhythm with her intonation. First, a slightly ascending tone—almost neutral—reflecting obligatory politeness: "thanks," avoiding eye contact. Then, like a dagger, a faintly rising tone, keeping me alive but devoid of hope: "see you." And finally, as her head turned to avoid meeting my gaze, a descending tone, signaling closure and the bare minimum of effort: "at work."

The audience around us—silent witnesses to this fleeting drama—watched her lips press ever so slightly, hinting at concealed frustration after seventeen minutes of poorly spent time. How fortunate I wasn't the screenwriter of my life—months later, when I finally confessed that embarrassing moment of insecurity born from my imagination, she simply locked her eyes on mine, her pupils brimming with humour. She laughed softly, shaking her head, and said, "That would never have happened."

As soon as my body stood fully upright, the joke my mind had conspired with my subconscious was condemned to ostracism by my right hand, which imperiously invaded her personal space, touching her left shoulder, while we maintained eye contact. My eyes, complicit, made a subtle gesture of greeting as my torso leaned towards her approximately 15 degrees from the waist, a soft, barely noticeable yet highly intentional movement, followed by my head turning 45 degrees to the left, exposing my cheek. My neck, which remained aligned for a fleeting instant, tilted 10 degrees towards her, leaving no space between our faces. The eye contact broke as her soft cheek became my new focal point—our faces, caressing each other for the first time.

The entire sequence unfolded fluidly within a span of two seconds, radiating courtesy and confidence—both of which were shattered when, in an immediate, natural reflex, I moved to give her a second kiss on her other cheek. However, the cultural absence of the double-kiss in her led her to skilfully turn her face without losing her composure. This produced a spark of exciting tension. At that moment, the director of my imagination—ever dramatic—lost his temper and shouted from the depths of his being: "CUT! BACK TO THE BEGINNING!"

From that point where no one could escape the sun's rays, I suggested we go have a drink—that was my idea of a date. During the walk to the pub I'd impulsively chosen, it felt as though our minds had entered a dressing room. There, expert makeup artists began removing the layers of our psyches. With great mastery, they applied a base of dopamine to smooth and unify, three strokes of adrenaline, noradrenaline, and serotonin to accentuate the shadows and the glow. The finishing touch came with a setting spray of oxytocin, not forgetting the lightest trace of cortisol eyeliner for a touch of naturalness. A quick review, a check under the light—"no corrections!" And after three blinks of our lashes against our lower lids, we were seated across from each other in the outdoor area of a harbour-facing pub.

As we sipped our first beer, my pupils expanded, letting in more of her light and capturing each of her exquisite features as if I were seeing her for the first time—features that, at first glance, seemed to hail from somewhere between the Strait of Gibraltar and Istanbul.

Her face was oval, with a jawline that seemed to have been gently chiselled, while her high, prominent cheekbones granted her elegance and symmetry. With two blinks, my emerald eyes jumped to hers. They were large, with a subtle tilt at the outer corners—there was something feline in them—and the amber of her irises gluttonously absorbed the day's brightness, while the sun's luminance filtered into my glass of beer—colours resembling fresh honey, not the bitter taste coursing through my throat with each sip. Her gaze was magnetic, exuding a sense of mystery—a mystery her long, thick lashes accentuated even more.

I stopped looking at her eyes to trace the defined bridge of her nose, which reinforced her symmetry, character and elegance. The softly rounded tip of her nose became the perfect springboard for my focus to land on her full, luscious, and perfectly defined lips—they were the very embodiment of sensual sin! Their rosy hue harmonised with her flawless skin, a light olive tone. The small beauty mole I had already noticed on the left side of her chin, paired with her well-defined, slightly arched eyebrows, completed my exploration.

Although her dark, extraordinarily long and voluminous hair wasn't technically part of her face, it framed her features beautifully, elevating each one of them. That hair carried with it the essence of vineyards, vibrant markets with Arab influences, and medieval villages perched on hills overlooking white-sand or golden beaches caressed by crystal-clear waters.

How wrong I had been! There was something unique in the brushstrokes that composed her Mediterranean presence; her beauty didn't belong to one place but to the confluence of many. I gained more clarity when she pulled me back to reality. "My Mum's from China, and my Dad's white," she said. Foolishly, I had been thinking of the Silk Road.

That afternoon, our impish tongues threw words like little stones randomly into the lake of time. Sitting here now as I write, on a distant shore from where we were, I trace their ripples etched onto the surface, transmitting fragments of memory. I don't clearly remember what came from our mouths that day, but I vividly recall the actions they set in motion.

It felt like a conspiracy—the sun, displeased at the highest point in the sky, frustrated at not being able to watch us completely. We had taken refuge under a parasol, shielding ourselves from its zenithal glow. Relentlessly, it advanced more aggressively in its diurnal cycle towards the horizon, settling into a more comfortable position to ensure it wouldn't miss a single one of our interactions. Enviously, its light kicked at the shadows cast by our beer glasses, stretching them across the table, as if to remind us of its presence. We, in turn, tried to push aside the banality of our conversation. Around us, voices faintly breathed, mingling with the heat of a dying summer, while my fingers brushed against hers, drawn to the scent of her dark perfume. Without meaning to, we began to play like children in a playground. What could be more fascinating than two souls surrendering to the innocence of childhood, daring to rediscover the world together? And yet, there was no place for innocence in that moment.

Our glasses began to sweat, watching as she and I risked it all in an old and dangerous game to see who would be the unfortunate loser and thus choose either to reveal something secret and sacred from their inner world or to bring a ridiculous action into the reality surrounding us. We were perfectly in sync within the private space we were constructing. I saw myself reflected in her pupils, and she didn't take her eyes off mine; not a single blink. The silence reigning in that instant was interrupted by the cough of some imaginary spectator. Our voices fused in unison, summoning our fate: "Rock! Paper! Scissors!" My gaze slowly shifted from the tips of her eyelashes to see her open hand covering my closed fist. The crowd roared in ecstatic delight. She revelled in her triumph, as if Caesar himself had decreed her victory. I closed my eyes, then looked up at her face, radiant with happiness, to accept my humiliating punishment.

"Truth," I declared, as the whiteness of her teeth blinded me.

Without breaking her gaze, she tilted her head slightly, as if savouring her victory. Then, her question came. It was direct, precise, and loaded with an unexpected weight that made the air around us tense.

"What's your biggest fear?"

My brain interpreted those words after receiving the electrical impulses that, moments earlier, had been sound waves travelling through the air, escaping her vocal cords, and making my eardrums vibrate.

She had been merciful; she had shown benevolence.

Without thinking and without breaking eye contact, I replied, "Dying before my mom and not writing a book before I die."

We fell silent for a moment.

She wasn't expecting that answer.

I didn't want to explain it.

Just before a second question could leap from her lips, one slipped from my tongue, smooth as a slide: "What about you? What's your biggest fear?" This caught her by surprise, but calmness was one of her traits. "I haven't lost," she nonchalantly responded. An invisible thread seemed to tug the right corner of her mouth upward.

The heavy air wasn't prepared for what was coming. A domino effect began innocently with a sip of beer, the intensity of our stares, our voices in unison, my mocking face, her squinting eyes, and a faint "fuck" escaping her lips, ending with my right hand covering her closed right fist. The roles shifted. Gallantly, without letting go of her fist, I moved my hand to surround hers. When I felt her fingers, I gently tugged, opening her hand as my eyelashes fluttered against the space between us, unconsciously trying to reach her. When only the tips of our fingerprints touched, I turned my hand again and pushed it towards her, intertwining our fingers. I glanced to the right, then slowly to the left, before meeting her eyes again. She seemed to read my mind. Out of nowhere, my smile betrayed her curiosity — I said "Would you kiss that man over there?"

It was a random guy sitting with his back to us, someone who had nothing to do with us. His face didn't matter; he was just part of our game. She tilted her head slightly, her free hand feeling the tips of her hair. Her laughter spilled out unexpectedly, catching even her off guard: "Of course not!"

We barely noticed how the next few minutes passed, as we were being carried by waves of laughter and coquettish glances, where our growing complicity kept us afloat. That's how the afternoon went on. The people around us were pawns in our game, with suppositions bordering on the ridiculous, each one escalating the tone and elevating our fun. She fit perfectly into the role—her imagination was provocative, and my impudence meshed seamlessly with her indomitable spirit.

"If that man over there offered you $10,000 for sex right now, what would you say?" I teased.

She didn't miss a beat. "No," she said, raising an eyebrow, "what about you?"

"Absolutely," I answered without hesitation, "but only so I could spend the money with you. Though you'd need to get me a lot of ice—he looks like a stallion."

I was an idiot, but it made her laugh.

There wasn't a single spot on her hands that didn't bear traces of mine, and vice versa.

I don't know why I said what I said, but it was something that had already been written in the stars, something that had already happened in our past lives and would happen again in the lives to come. A small crack in the fabric of reality had formed—the light in the depths of her pupils had granted me a new perspective on my identity. The din of sounds surrounding us was torn by my voice: "Do you want to be my girlfriend for six hours?" I could hear the pounding of my own heart echoing against hers. It seemed as though no physical bodies separated us. The wind itself had stopped, waiting for her answer. The sun blushed, painting the sky with fire, as she, without hesitation, replied, "Yes."

Her glistening lips captured all my attention. We pulled towards each other. I didn't want to close my eyes, but gradually, everything else faded. My hands felt the softness of her hair, her nose grazed mine, our eyelashes danced together. My lips pressed against her upper lip; hers caressed my lower one. In an instant, the rhythm shifted, and my tongue traced the delicate curves of her full lower lip.

Our tongues met.

"Hello."

"Hola."

What a fucking fantastic moment.

As soon as my breath parted from hers, somewhere between the harbour and the murmurs of the place, an invisible finger pressed an imaginary key. Reality shifted its rhythm with a soft "click", and minimalist musical waves burst around us, a hypnotic, repetitive beat that submerged us into a music video.

The camera focused on two women, between 45 and 50 years old, watching us from the other table. Envy was drawn on their faces—a lament for the excess of someone else's passion. A funky bassline with a catchy rhythm entered. What we had seemed like an accidental performance, as private as it was public. The cameraman wasted no time and zoomed in on our faces: lips moving, synchronised in silence as the music drowned out our words.

Close-up—my hand hovering over the table, moving towards hers, as if gravity had been weakened by a synth pad, cuts of the same movement but in different backgrounds, like predicting the future, reinforcing warmth and adding a nostalgic air.

Low-angle shot—my slow steps, hers echoing in sync, a cut showing my back as I urinated, another cut: her in the bathroom putting on make-up, her reflection in the mirror meeting mine from the adjacent sink. The intrusive cameraman zooming in on her smile as I opened the door.

A kiss.

Now on the street, the bass resonated through the trees, speeding up the world around us. Every corner became an excuse: I pushed her gently against the walls, my hands seeking the curve of her hips and moving lower to cup her ass, her fingers clinging to my neck, pulling me towards her with the same urgency. The camera spun in circles, capturing us from above—elongated shadows projected onto the pavement, sunlight chasing us—a "white noise" that rose progressively, building tension and marking the arrival of the drop. Her brown eyes locked on my green irises, cars passing by in a blur, as if we were the only ones with the right to exist in that moment.

Another cut. The bass and percussion dominated everything, while my hand was filmed opening the door to the room with force, then the snap of a beer can. Foam burst forth as if the music's energy controlled it, spilling while we tore at each other's clothes. A blue light enveloped us, making everything more intimate, more unreal. I kissed her abdomen; her nails dug into my back, leaving indelible marks only I could feel. The camera grew chaotic—rapid, blurry movements capturing the trembling of the bed. A close-up: my mouth on her rosy nipples, her mouth open in ecstasy, flashes of sweat under the light, and the wild synchronisation of two bodies that remembered each other.

The music kept blasting, windows vibrating, guitar accents, every bass hit feeding the rhythm of our movements. In a suspended moment, the camera slowly pulled away—the blue light turning red, our shadows dancing on the wall. The song began to unravel, the bass disappearing, the camera zooming in on the old chandelier with a single light bulb. The track faded, leaving a fade-out, a final echo in the melody. Reality was gasping, she and I two spectres joined by something beyond time and space, the same invisible finger pressing the key—pause."

Curiously, the phrase "The old chandelier with a single bulb" nestled at the end of that over-verbose writing was what—twenty years ago—made me feel as if something were watching me while I read. What a singular image I have of that moment: my eyes lifting off the screen, my head turning to the right, the faint light emanating from the solitary bulb dragging me into the story, breaking the barrier between fiction and reality. My face tensed under the weight of doubt, my gaze returned to the screen, focusing on the phrase—imagining the stranger who wrote it sitting where I was, tapping the keys, our hearts beating in unison on two purple nights separated by time.

In the blink of an eye, I leapt from thoughts of the past to the present as I rested my elbows on the desk, interlacing my fingers, my lips softly pressed against them. That memory began to dissolve languidly into a stream of justifications: some branching over time, others stagnant in their flow. I know it was pure coincidence that I found the USB; it wasn't left for me to discover. Perhaps it wasn't even left for anyone to find. It was an accident—like my arrival at that room, or even that city. Who uses a USB in 2024?

An accident, like staying in a hostel for two days surrounded by backpackers and homeless people. Like feeling disgusted by the lack of cleanliness and becoming desperate to apply for every available room in the city. Like receiving an email asking when I wanted to inspect one. Like barely looking at the place and telling the agent I wanted to take it as soon as possible. Like her telling me I could move in that very day if I paid the deposit. Like being handed the keys that same afternoon. Like me, distracted, exploring the empty room, opening the second drawer of the white desk and finding, in a corner, something that didn't belong to the room but had been part of someone else's life.

The contents of the USB, however, didn't stir anything in me at first. It was the story of an ordinary man living an ordinary life, a bit too old to be washing dishes and dating women so young. You must live in an orgasmic void to dream up such demented colours. I thought it wasn't worth continuing. I copied the file onto my laptop just in case, and left the inert thing in the drawer, gathering dust alongside the trash of the days. My life continued as before: light, full of unfulfilled promises that youth allowed me to delay. The house, though functional, hid in its corners the reflection of those who inhabited it: cordial, sometimes indifferent greetings; a routine marked by the constant smell of curry and superficial coexistence with others. The privacy I valued was interrupted one night by screams coming from a neighbouring room.

"For fuck's sake! Oh, come on, motherfucker!"

The hoarse voice, laden with a nasal accent, echoed—breaking the fragile tranquillity of the night. At first, I ignored it. But when the screams persisted for three more nights, my curiosity—or perhaps my discomfort—led me to inquire with the other inhabitants. A very polite Japanese woman, whose name I can't recall, told me that the man in the room beneath mine suffered from some mental disability, and that the state, instead of offering him proper treatment, had left him to his own devices with a weekly pension and a medical prescription. She also told me, unprompted, that the previous occupant of my room had repeatedly complained about this situation.

That's when I realised that my inaction had allowed the screams to continue. The first time I took an example from that stranger was when I sent an email to the agency that very morning. As if by magic, the screams stopped that night.

I don't know if it was that silent connection with the former tenant, or accumulated curiosity, that led me to reopen the file copied from the USB onto my laptop. Something compelled me to reread it. This time, the words carried a different weight. I remembered the sensation of that first night—my mind migrating from the present to the past, imagining the stranger sitting in that same chair, tapping the keys under the faint glow of a solitary bulb.

On that distinct night, the wind brushed against the windows, amplifying the warmth and protection of the walls around me. The heaviness in my eyes overpowered the pull of insomnia, as the blurred letters faded between soft blinks. Fragmented images of blue and red lights replaced the sickly yellow glow that enveloped me. I was no longer seated. Without perceiving the movement, I found myself standing at the edge of my bed. A thin mist bathed the scene before me, softening its shapes yet failing to obscure the two bodies entwined on the mattress. Ethereal murmurs and gasps filled the air, their rhythm inviting me to sit at the foot of the bed. My weightless body obeyed without hesitation.

Slowly, I leaned back, propping myself up on my left elbow. My gaze fell on the strands of hair cascading over a slender, bare back.

A hand gripped those strands imperiously while another was viciously stroking the contours of the woman's ass. Her nails scraped his chest as they moved to an unrelenting rhythm, a tide I was powerless to escape. Voyeuristic fascination held me captive. A secret within me emerged, avowing the unavowable—impossible to resist.

My arm extended, and my fingertips brushed against the veins on his masculine hand. Electricity coursed through me—a visceral reaction to the contact. My fingers slid across his, then ventured lower, trailing the curve of her soft body. Androgynous pleasure, for an instant I felt their mouths tasting me. The scene broke as they turned to face me. His eyes locked onto mine with piercing intensity, and she, her head tilting back, met my gaze with a weary, blissful expression. As soon as this happened, their gazes jolted me—as if a snake had struck me—poison running through me.

My head snapped upright, and I found myself seated once more in front of the computer screen. The clammy weight of my eyelids, and the lingering warmth in my loins, told me it had been more than a simple dream.

A dream I still visualise, one that hasn't lost its colour, with different interpretations moulded by the years—a back-and-forth motion. Did it awaken or reveal something in me? My soul had shrieked that night, "Was I drawn to them, to him, or to her?" The boundaries of my desires felt porous, undefined, leaving me unsettled but oddly alive. Reflecting on this, my hand reaches for the glass of water. I take a slow sip, observing the lines and wrinkles on my hands, the faint sunspots, and the more prominent veins—time's markings.

They shout at me, their echoes reflected in the sculpted features of my face, that none of this could have been accidental.

What would have been accidental would have been not giving more importance to it—not trying to find out more about who might have written it.

The text had given me a few clues: the nameless author mentioned that he had started writing it on a Friday, 30 August. The year wasn't specified, but I easily deduced it was the current one,—2024. The last Friday that fell on 30 August before that year had been in 2019.

This small deduction should have been enough to convince me that the "writer" was the previous occupant of my room. However, a bland doubt lingered in my mind: what if it wasn't him?

That uncertainty led me to seek more information from my housemates that same morning.

It feels so embarrassing now, remembering how I behaved then. But it wasn't entirely my fault. The interactions were so dull. I made my best effort to fully engage my social battery, breaking the ice, my mouth awkwardly smiling as I dropped weightless greetings alongside crumbs of pastry softly falling to the floor while I drank coffee in the shared living room.

Two or three people, headphones in, eating something quickly before heading to work—interrupted by my presence. Awkward exchanges limped along until they died in the agony of my response: "I'm going to start university next year; I came early to settle in, get to know the place, and avoid setbacks."

The same lie I had told my father—and that, at the time, was my only truth.

Thankfully, the people in the house showed only shallow interest, just like me.

Frustration simmered beneath the surface. I couldn't find the right moment—nor an excuse—to ask what I wanted. Each attempt felt clumsy until, mercifully, they said their goodbyes and left. Annoyed, I left the house for a walk, hoping clarity would strike as the sky began to split. Raindrops fell alongside the crumbs of my croissant, smearing my thoughts across the pavement.

That same afternoon, upon returning home and opening the heavy door to the kitchen, I found the Japanese woman who lived in the room opposite mine. I greeted her and, although I had already eaten out, I decided to "make myself some tea."

She was focused on preparing her dinner—or whatever it was—her quick and precise movements revealing a practiced skill. I decided to intrude on her focused labour, mentioning my complaint to the real estate agency, saying it had worked, in a tone that mimicked gratitude.

She paid attention to me, though her responses were short, enough to show courtesy without real interest.

The conversation didn't flow. I observed her black hair and her deliberate movements, which seemed calculated.

I shared a little about myself—a monologue, though I didn't have much to tell. Essentially, I repeated the lie I had told others earlier that morning.

To my surprise, she had studied at the same university, which allowed us to discuss trivialities. When I felt the moment was right, I asked about the person who had lived in my room before me.

There was a pause.

After thinking for a moment, she admitted that she didn't know much about him.

"He was unpredictable," she said. "Sometimes very sociable, almost full of energy—a bit cheeky. Other times, he was quiet and reserved, to the point of being rude, as if the people around him didn't exist."

She added that she had lived in the house for a year, and that the previous tenant had already been there when she arrived.

"He left suddenly last month, mid-November. Someone—I don't know who—came and packed up his things. Then the real estate agent started showing the room to new tenants."

Apparently, it wasn't unusual for this to happen in the house—people came and went, not forming any real bonds. Everyone lived their own reality.

Why had he disappeared? Who had collected his belongings? Was it him? Was it someone else? Why did they leave the USB behind?

Caravans of questions swirled in my head, growing louder as she continued.

"He was Latin American," she added, almost as an afterthought. "His name was Victor."

I froze, thanked her, and withdrew to my room, leaving her to her culinary meditation.

My mind was alight with speculation. That night, I returned to the text.

III

51

"Hysterical Solitude watched us from the edge of the bed; it had borne silent witness to everything. Jealousy burned in its eyes, fixed on our trembling bodies. It breathed in the stench of our fresh juices, our tongues intertwined as we tangled in strands of her hair. We ignored it completely. It went mad, feeling betrayed—it was unforgivable.

As my "Enemiga's" warm breath caressed my neck, I turned to Solitude with a defiant smile. Mysteriously, this action brought it back to its senses. It gazed at me with pity, laughing bitterly. For a fleeting moment, my actions had made it doubt itself. But Solitude knew it was indispensable. If I abandoned it, I would place the entire burden on the one resting in my arms—and like a dog, I would inevitably return, tail between my legs.

Cold and calculating, it leans in close and whispers with tenderness in my ear as I write now: "You didn't know how to use me."

Before my finger pressed the key that started this paragraph, its words made me look away from the screen. In response, I stared at it blankly.

It held my gaze with arrogance, the faint light in my cornea reflecting its figure. It didn't like that. Its cold fingers gripped my chin, and it came so close that it eclipsed all incoming light. I didn't blink as I felt it exploring the darkness of my pupil. It laughed disdainfully because, deep within that vast darkness, it saw how faint lights began to flicker, reclaiming some space in the shadows. It felt trapped in a microcosm of sensations and subtle changes. Without seeing anyone around, it perceived constant murmurs, hushed laughter, soft conversations, and the intrusive crackle of plastic wrappers. The atmosphere of anticipation had swallowed it. Suddenly, the light from a screen burst forth, illuminating its face and revealing expressions of attention, curiosity, and fascination that it hadn't expected. For a beat, silence took over everything. A ceremonial moment before images, encapsulated in the deepest corners of my mind, began to unspool like a film reel: me, watching my enemiga naked before me, dressing slowly without a trace of shame. Her accomplice, the sunlight, poured through the window, beckoning us to step outside so it could greet us again. We agreed without hesitation. She and I walked towards another bar, traces of passion lingering in her beautiful, dishevelled hair. The marks of her kisses still burned on my neck. Every deserted street was ours, filled with complicity.

The taste of her sweat lingered on the tip of my tongue, my throat still bathed in her sweet fluids. One, two, three beers. The two of us taking a photo in front of a dirty mirror in some bar, our reflections blurred yet intimately connected. Our hands intertwined as we returned to my place that night, the moon at its zenith, our silent voyeur, stealing her attention with every step.

She and I, naked in my bed.

Sleeping together as if we had always known each other.

Coffee in the morning.

She went back home.

Me sighing incredulous, in this same spot.

The two of us meeting again as strangers at our workplace, pretending the night had never happened, she like a succubus visiting me every night that week.

A mocking smile crept across the demanding cinephile's face as the images rolled on. It couldn't contain its laughter and, out of respect, withdrew—not without first reminding me that nothing lasts forever, that every joy is borrowed, and, sadly, every connection is fleeting.

What began as a fling quickly mutated. She repeatedly told me she didn't like the idea of a relationship—she radiated freedom, independence, and rebellion. I didn't say anything; things just happened. It's one thing to summon the devil, another to see him appear. The 15-year gap that separated us was nothing but an aphrodisiac. We talked endlessly, developing our own language, seeing each other almost every day, going on "clandestine" trips, and our lungs burst at concerts chanting "we must never be apart." Oh, the irony. I got sick in her arms, she in mine. We smoked. Whisky, gin, and coffee were our allies. Baron de Charlus made us laugh with his august humour.

One day I found a note from her resting on my bed: "Te amo, the sun shines a little brighter today because you fucked me so good last night."

And did I enjoy it? ¡Jueputa, sí! Of course I did.

Those were some of the best days I'd had in years — reckless, vivid without shame, full of unprecedented, limitless plans. Together we were the best team, tearing conventions apart like paper.

One night, after too many drinks at a bar, we walked under the shadows of the trees. The cold bit into our skin, but her presence — her breath — was warmer than anything I'd ever known. The night was heavy with silence, save for the occasional murmur of distant cars. The moon clung to her gaze, casting a soft silver glow that made her seem untouchable.

It felt like a dream. Me the dreamer inside her dreams—or she, within mine.

I didn't kiss her. Not right away. My eyes held hers as if searching for something beyond what either of us could comprehend. They sparkled, reflecting a faint light, her breathing heavy but calm. The tension thickened the air between us. Her eyelids fluttered slowly, like the lazy wings of a beautiful bird, spent from flight. My gaze followed the line of her lips, the soft contours of her skin. I knew what I had to do. This would define everything.

"Do you want to be my girlfriend?" My voice broke the stillness, confident but not demanding.

Before she could answer, a car sped by, its headlights cutting through the darkness, shattering the fragile glass of the perfect night. For a moment, the beams of light painted her in orgasmic colours, as if reality itself had paused to give her a cosmic frame. Particles of light fell like rain.

And then it came—a soft, almost imperceptible "yes." I didn't let the word linger in the air. My lips found hers, stealing her answer, devouring it completely. My wet tongue met hers, drawing us closer, binding us in that moment.

We were two imperfect words at the end of a twisted verse—rhythmic but unrhymed, within an unnecessary stanza. It was laden with incongruent metaphors and tangled similes, yet it formed part of a delirious poem.

From that moment on, our journey through the galaxy began accelerating faster and faster. Clearly, everything has its cycle. I stayed at the same place, no longer washing dishes—I had been promoted to other culinary tasks, climbing slowly but steadily. Meanwhile, she left, finding something better, something that gave more value to her days. She was always reaching for more, her ambitions endless, her steps sure and deliberate. And yet, despite the distance her departure might have implied, our relationship didn't falter.

There were no fights or arguments; with each passing moon, we seemed to challenge gravity, creating new and more exciting plans—even she decided to learn the Cervantes' language. But as we hurtled forward, the overwhelming speed made me cling to her more and more. For me, it seemed normal—a natural side effect of love. But as Gemini reached its peak and the waxing gibbous moon turned into a full moon at 3:41 a.m., its silver light revealed something I had tried to ignore. It was something unsettling to my ex-enemiga, something that defied her independent nature: a face distorted by dependence.

My face.

Though Mercury was in Taurus, favouring practical and reflective communication, and Venus in Cancer intensified emotions and sensitivity in relationships, it wasn't enough to make up for what she had seen. Under this celestial influence, she sent me a text message saying she needed time and space. The expected excuse: our difference in ages. I responded with a playful yet composed tone, assuring her that I understood and respected her august wishes; it wasn't maturity speaking — it was the red planet in Leo, lending energy and enthusiasm to my actions.

What a fucking sadness.

Our trajectory through that Milky Way gradually began to diverge. It was a very tough moment, but there was a promise that we would meet again at some point in the cosmos. Those were cold, empty months, illuminated only by occasional flickers — like stars dying in the distance.

Eleven days before Virgo's reign would fall, Aphrodite was in Leo, amplifying the expression of love and creativity. For that very reason, I had received a message from my ex-enemiga asking me to step outside and look at the waning moon in Cancer adorning the night sky. I hesitated for a second before acting; Zeus retrograde in Taurus suggested that I ought to introspect on personal growth instead — the day, by all accounts, demanded it. But then Cronus retrograde in Pisces whispered that I should trust my intuition.

I rose abruptly, my chair tearing the rug, and within three steps, I was at the door to my room. Clumsily, I slipped on my shoes. My body felt light as I reached the threshold that separated my house from the street. With each heartbeat, my movements grew heavier, weighted with meaning. Violins began to play high, sustained notes that seemed to slice through the air. The bow scraped the strings nervously, mirroring my hand as it turned the doorknob. Both the violin and I seemed to be holding our breath.

The rhythm quickened, the tension rose. The music climbed in ascending glissandos, like a serpent climbing my spine. My mind screamed, "Step outside! Don't hesitate motherfucker!, do it quickly!" Yet my movements became controlled, deliberate, when I caught her scent. That perfume—a narcotic aroma of jasmine interwoven with the dark, spiced woodiness of liquor. It exuded unapologetic sensuality, a feminine confidence that reveled in its audacity. It was intoxicating, and I couldn't resist.

Nonchalantly, I stepped out onto the street, slowly turning my head left, then right. There was no one. Only the moon, a celestial voyeur with one face shrouded in shadow and the other radiant with light. I felt watched, and when I lowered my gaze, I saw it: a black package tied with a red ribbon. I opened it right there on the street. Inside was an old copy of Raskolnikov's torment, once again in my hands, along with another book. I flipped it open to the first page, where a note was inscribed: "Feliz cumpleaños, mi amor..." ending with "You're forever mine."

Borges saw my trembling lower lip after reading it, the earthquake I held back within myself, the echo of her lingering in the ink of that note. He saw me, frozen in a single second that stretched into eternity. He saw her too, dissolving into my fantasies of seeing her that night, merging with the constellations hanging above me.

He saw it all—within the Aleph.

My mind had been sedated for 25 days and 24 nights until the fourteenth day of Libra arrived. That morning, I found myself in a predicament: the absolute absence of mariachis in this part of the world—leaving me with only one option. At 7:57 a.m., I grabbed my phone and called my beloved.

One, two, three rings. Her breathing on the line. My voice turning raspier and deeper than usual, a slight Mexican accent accompanied by a forced vibrato, using my throat instead of my diaphragm to sing "Las Mañanitas." All the Aztecs and Maya surely rolled in their graves. She broke into uncontrollable laughter, cracking the heavens, listening bewildered, with no idea what was happening.

I said, seamlessly switching languages, "Feliz cumpleaños," "Joyeux anniversaire," "Happy birthday." Her smile licked my ears as she responded "thank you." I confidently proposed that we go to Sydney together: a music festival, jumping out of a fucking plane, spending New Year's Eve at a sick party.

She said yes, I said "te amo"; she echoed back "I love you." I hung up. My heart buoyant with certainty that Mercury in Virgo had blessed my words with analytical precision. I was dying to share that night's waning gibbous moon with her—but I knew I had to wait.

I wish I could jump from that birthday phone call straight to the divine morning when I would wake up knowing I'd see her again, but that leap is only possible in the realm of storytelling. In real life, there were fucking, agonisingly slow, drawn-out months.

The constant focus on the future—my mind trapped in the question "What's going to happen?"—kept me from messaging her too often. But every time one of her messages reached me, the epinephrine and norepinephrine released by my adrenal glands made my heart race. I'd read the message; a sudden calm would wash over me. My mind bribed itself, imagining exaggerated scenarios. I trusted her blindly, so much so that the idea of her not showing up that day never even crossed my mind.

It was a contradiction. The months turned into weeks. The sensation of inevitability breathing down my neck. A sacred, electric tension flooded my body with hormones. As if that weren't enough, in the final days leading up to it, time around me seemed to speed up while I remained static, images blurring as I moved through my daily actions. Words hanging in the air.

There was a party in my brain, a chemical dance between excitement and stress taking centre stage. Motivation and fear, completely intoxicated, got into a fistfight. The uproar grew so intense that my nucleus accumbens lit up the night before the day I'd been waiting for, releasing dopamine. There was some uncertainty, but very little. That night, I slept like never before—I was both utterly drained and brimming with energy.

I knew it wasn't a dream. I felt a faint warmth behind my eyelids, a luminous pressure seeping through as if the light were pleading with me to open them, hysterically insistent. When I cracked them open, it smacked me awake. I watched as my eyelashes seemed to evaporate under the intense light that felt as though it were pushing reality inward. Each blink was a fleeting reprieve, an attempt to stave off the inevitable, but the light persisted, growing brighter with each breath, flooding my field of vision with an unrelenting white.

In that moment, I felt what Anna must have felt in Tsarist Russia. Except my light wasn't a train; it was the consequence of forgetting to close the curtains the night before.

The day I had longed for had finally arrived.

Our meeting was set for 5:27 p.m. at the airport. The flight was scheduled at 7:30 p.m. Naturally, I had offered that we leave together from my place, but she firmly declined, insisting it would be better to meet at the airport entrance. I accepted, relishing the tension this decision generated.

After finishing my daily tasks and packing a small suitcase, I decided to take a second shower. I needed it. As soon as I undressed, I felt compelled to open the small bathroom window. I knew someone from the street might catch a glimpse of me, but they'd only see my perfectly shaved scalp gleaming under the midday light. I turned the hot water on, waiting until steam had completely taken over my surroundings.

It was summer—a masochistic act, but a necessary one.

The scalding water first licked the nape of my neck, streaming down my back—not broad but well-defined. Rivulets left faint red marks on the slightly sun-kissed white skin of my trapezius muscles as they slid down my spine, reaching my slender waist. My firm, proportioned glutes sent stray droplets ricocheting against the tiled walls, while the more lustful streams traced the roundness of my buttocks before gliding down the ischial muscles of my thighs.

When I fully stepped under the cascade, I closed my eyes, feeling the heavy pull of my damp eyelashes. My high cheekbones and full lips stoically received the first scorching streams of water. But why say the water was scorching or burning if it were merely hot? Perhaps something within me had grown more sensitive to the external world, magnifying what it had to offer.

I inhaled deeply, the steam carrying faint traces of water molecules, while the boldest streams carved paths over my rounded shoulders, their descent onto my masculine chest akin to candle wax dripping intentionally in sadistic pleasure.

I'd be a liar if I didn't confess that the water kissed the clear lines of my abs with equal fervour. Neither the hairs on my tattooed arms, nor the muscles in my legs, nor even my toenails escaped this savage, voluptuous journey.

I am a conceited idiot, but the water seemed to leave hotter than it came after licking my heels, carrying part of me down the drain. I remember opening my eyes and feeling a profound release—my muscles relaxed, an internal warmth spreading with tingling sensations from my pelvic region to every corner that my veins and arteries could reach.

In one word: plenitude.

My vision focused on the droplets of water condensed on the glass. As they fused, they slid down at great speed, some pushing others that had been at rest, accelerating their movement and leaving streaks on the fogged glass—patterns and textures, countless paths, all ending in the same place where parts of me had already vanished with the water.

I was fucking clean, but not innocent.

There were six hours left until I would see her. Life felt utterly wonderful in that moment.

I had everything planned. I would approach her confidently, seeing her smile as she spotted me, both of us dressed in black, the moment I stepped through the first airport door at 5:26 p.m., subsequent to having taken 17 steps from the bus after thanking the driver, after sitting in the last seat on the right with my head resting against the glass, feeling the vibrations that lulled me, after boarding the bus at 4:50 p.m., immediately after waiting 2-minutes and 45 seconds, which came after a 12-minute and 7-second walk from where I am writing this right now, after having finished gathering my documents and double-checking the message she had sent me at 2:46 p.m., a message that had erased any doubt—any trace of uncertainty—that I would see her that day.

Precisely 8 seconds after 4:35 p.m., I took my first step towards the bus stop. As soon as I began walking, I put on my headphones, and without delay, Gahan's intense, elegant and magnetic voice coursed through my nervous system. The journey began with "Stripped" (4:18), followed by "Enjoy the Silence" (4:22). The route became flooded with sexy electronic music, saturated with darkness and melancholy. Three seconds after "Walking in My Shoes" (6:12) ended, I was already boarding the bus. I paused the music to greet the driver and show him my ticket. I walked down the aisle and sat in the last seat on the right.

The bus started moving.

Six hundred-and-fifty-seven metres later, it slowed down to pick up more passengers at the next stop. My eyes were fixed on the street while my mind wandered among the stars when, suddenly, I recognised a familiar shape in the distance boarding the bus. It was her. Her beautiful hair was loose, much longer than before. She wasn't dressed entirely in black but wore her unmistakable boots. Her skin looked paler, but as she approached, my heart felt like it was about to burst out of my chest, like a dog waiting all day for its owner to come home.

I stood up without taking my eyes off her. No words came out of my mouth. I reached for her hand and gave her space to sit by the window. She sat down, never breaking her gaze. I sat down, never breaking mine. The driver, watching us from the rear-view mirror, did not take his eyes off us either.

Her presence stripped away my abstractions, forcing me into the raw immediacy of the now. The weight of the months we had spent apart evaporated, replaced by a visceral clarity.

All I could feel was her.

She was beside me again. I don't know what I said to her. I don't know what she said. All I know is that as soon as the bus started moving, we kissed. I took her hands; we exchanged sacred words. The plan hadn't gone as I had envisioned. There weren't 17 steps, but there was a shared "thank you" to the driver.

We entered the airport, passed through security, and I playfully nudged her. She looked at me and laughed. Impish nonsense poured from my mouth. We shared a coffee, at 7:29 p.m. we boarded the plane—it was quick and beautiful.

Unforgettable.

Our seats were in the rear-left section of the plane. Without giving me a chance to think, she asked for the window seat. My natural reaction was to feign surprise and firmly say, "No," grabbing her hand before letting her pass with a smirk. I placed our carry-on luggage in the overhead compartment and took my seat beside her.

The usual routine followed: people finding their seats, a calm and professional voice resonating through the speakers, instilling confidence and tranquillity to the passengers. Small children cried in the arms of distracted parents—the closer the child, the sharper and more irritating the tone. The flight attendants, unbothered and serene, demonstrated the safety protocols, while my hand toyed idly with hers.

The plane began taxiing towards the runway. At that time of year, dusk fell around 8:52 p.m. As the aircraft started to take off, the sun could be seen dressed in red in the background of the window she had claimed. The few clouds on the horizon looked like cotton stained with blood, and a faint orange light encapsulated our irises as the plane's wheels slowly lifted off the ground, retracting to improve aerodynamic efficiency. Our voices merged with the roar of the engines; even though we hadn't seen each other for months, it felt as though only a few hours had passed. We spoke about the things we would do once we landed at 9:10 p.m. The past wasn't mentioned, nor what had happened in our lives during those months of absence from each other.

Through that tiny window, we could see the immensity of the ocean and without realising it, after separating for a brief kiss and opening our eyes, night had already enveloped the plane. But internally, all the darkness that had consumed me for months was mitigated by traces of light piercing tiny points in the void. As the streams of brightness penetrated, they expanded, like the reverse effect of a magnifying glass. I clung to the idea that, eventually, this light would rival the void, the darkness, the nothingness—this metaphysical force that had already staked its inevitable claim.

As we neared Sydney, the ground illuminated with countless lights that humiliated the starless sky. Once again, the voice from the speakers informed us we'd be landing in ten minutes. During those ten minutes, I let my body surrender to absolute repose, as if I had been submerged in warm water. I closed my eyes—I don't know if she closed hers—but I took her hand and kissed it. I could not explain what mental process drove me to do that.

The plane touched down, and the sound of the engines was overthrown by the multitude of passenger voices. We waited for most people to disembark, leaving almost last. As we descended the stairs from the plane, I caught myself imagining that the flashing lights around us were paparazzi cameras."

IV

"The long corridors of that colossal terminal were caressed by our footsteps until we reached the stairs leading to the underground train. Before crossing the ticket gate, I suddenly tugged her hand, and in a conspiratorial tone, leaned towards her. Her eyes, bright and curious, matched the sparkle escaping her mischievous smile as she whispered "What's up?". I reached into the back pocket of my pants and pulled out two debit cards—cards that bore no trace of my name. Relics of a past that had conveniently fallen into my prodigious hands. They were destined for this moment.

It was a silly thing, but I wanted to save the ticket fee for entering the station—50 bucks meant extra petrol for our nights—and if possible, avoid paying for transportation in the city altogether. I placed one of the cards in her hand, and she, my perfect accomplice, simply pushed her full lips into a pixieish pout, signalling complete understanding. We could have easily paid for each ticket. We could have just tapped the gate once and walked through together. Hell, we could have lifted a leg and hopped over the turnstile. There wasn't a single guard in sight. But no—we tapped simultaneously, passing through the gates like seasoned grifters: quick, subtle, and without incident.

Somewhere between three and ten minutes later, the train heading to Central Station arrived, and from there, we would take another train to Newtown, where I had booked a room in a pub for our first night. The ride was calm and uneventful, marked by the lights slicing through the darkness outside the windows and the robotic voice announcing the name of each stop as our conversation unfolded with absurd creativity. Taking advantage of our exotic features, we would claim to be from some Slavic country. My Latin American accent could hide in the shadow of her fluent English but with a comical yet convincing Russian accent. Her name: Svetlana. Of course, we were siblings from the same mother but different fathers, and if anyone questioned our overly affectionate behaviour? The best response: we enjoyed incest.

By the time we reached Newtown, we were giddy with laughter, walking into the pub where a man in a Hawaiian shirt—more eye-bags than person—handed us the key to our room, gave us directions on how to find it, and, of course, offered us a beer.

The beer disappeared into our systems like magic. We couldn't help but laugh when we noticed that each room in this "hotel" was named after a famous New York neighbourhood. Ours was Bushwick. From the name, I had expected some nod to urban art and emerging culture, but that was asking too much for $130 a night.

The room was simple: a bed, a fan, a wall-mounted television, a kettle, and a box of tea. There were no strange smells or noticeable stains on the sheets. The shared bathrooms were "la cereza en el pastel." It was fucking perfect.

As soon as we entered, the first thing I did was drop my backpack and press the light switch. As the light gained strength, I took a step forward and leapt onto the bed with my arms wide open. The mattress welcomed me softly, and as soon as my face rested on its surface, I caught a pleasant scent of lavender. Rolling over, I watched the slow blades of the fan spinning to the left. I closed my eyes and then opened them, looking towards the doorway. She remained upright, framed between the dim hallway and the halogen glow of the room.

She stepped forward and, without breaking focus, pushed the door gently with her left hand, pulling it back slightly, and sealed the room with a firm stomp of her left boot. The faint click of the latch framed the suspense with a clean, minimalist tone—almost imperceptible—yet it grew slowly. Her backpack settled on the floor with a muted grace. Her second step produced a lingering resonance that enveloped everything. Her eyes never left mine, and every blink from either of us drew us closer.

I felt as though the bed had become part of my body when the edge of it was touched by her right knee. Motionless, I waited as her left hand settled near my face, her hair cascading like waterfalls, sealing the space between her breath and mine. The almost imperceptible sound of her lips as she licked them was interrupted by a distant noise from the street, a harmonic shift in the air that created a fleeting lapse in focus. My right hand crept to the back of her neck, unnoticed, and my fingers wove into her hair, feigning nonchalance, nearly winding it around my wrist. I pulled her head gently back, her half-closed eyes gazing beyond the ether.

Mesmerised by her slender neck, I raised myself slightly so the tip of my nose could graze just beneath her ear, feeling the cold metal of her earrings brush my eyelashes, followed by the warmth of her earlobe. I sniffed the final line of her jaw before kissing her chin warmly. Pulling her head back a little more, following the rhythm of her breath, I traced discreet bites down to her collarbones.

She lowered her gaze from the stars to meet mine, and I loosened my grip on her hair. The collision of our lips fogged the windows.

With my left arm, I embraced her, pressing her entire body against mine. Her soft breasts rested against my chest, nearly interrupting the beat of my heart. Her hands cradled my face as if it were the Holy Grail, and I felt her languidly licking my lips. The taste of her sweet saliva transported me to the past, and a playful bite brought me back to the present.

Even as her prey, my hand had already slipped into her pants, feeling the firmness of her skin interrupted by the slight pressure imprinted by the fabric of her thong. I imagined flooding those lines with my breath. Slowly, she pulled her face away from mine, and her expression filled with mischief. Without a word, I removed my hand from the warmth of her ass and placed it on her waist. A volcano on the verge of eruption throbbed in my groin.

She felt it.

She looked at me provocatively, her hands already working on my leather belt. I toyed with the ends of her long hair. She took a breath, bit her lip, and, point-blank, shot: "I'm going to take a shower."

It sent me soaring.

With a playful "OK," I jumped off the bed, circled her like a cat, and kissed her neck, whispering in Spanish what her powerful game had stirred in me. She laughed conspiratorially, grabbed something from her suitcase and a towel, and turned her back to me.

Opening the door, she disappeared into the dim light outside, leaving me alone in Bushwick. I let myself fall backward onto the bed, agonising with pleasure as I stared once more at the fan blades spinning to the left.

I remained still for a minute or two. Faithful insomnia, a constant trait of my life, seemed to have abandoned me. The tranquillity I felt overflowed through every pore of my skin. I could have sworn that when she opened the door again, hours had passed—so much so that it might have already been the next day. This thought jolted me, and my drowsy eyes traced the shape of her body, wrapped tightly in the towel. Tiny droplets of water resting on her delicate shoulders smiled at me flirtatiously. Her face glowed, and the chignon she wore gave her an air of elegance and poise, though a rebellious strand of hair slid across her forehead.

From the bed, I enthusiastically said we should go find a party—it was still early. She slowly said she liked the idea.

My mind whispered: take off the towel.

She said: I need privacy.

The room answered for me: that's not possible here.

Candidly, I offered that if she wanted, I could turn around while she changed or did whatever she needed to do. She laughed softly, probably thinking: what an adorable idiot.

Without another word, I turned around and buried my head in the pillow. The towel slid silently to the floor.

"You can't look," she ordered, her voice playful. "I have a surprise for you."

"I promise not to look," I replied.

The fan sighed softly, as if it couldn't resist her nakedness.

The invisible echo of my thoughts collided with her silent and meticulous movements. Consonants and vowels released from her mouth broke the spell. I carefully released the pressure suffocating the pillow and, without opening my eyes, turned over. The first blink captured the light of the scene; my corneas, lenses, and retinas focused on her. She wore a short black Bardot dress, tight against her body. It perfectly framed the slenderness of her devilish figure, her bare shoulders pointed towards Alpha Centauri, and her firm breasts were an affront to morality, while the long sleeves preached mystery. Her hair, woven into a braid, freed only two rebellious strands that pointed towards her red-painted lips. Sleek lines extended the feline elegance of her eyes. An image frozen in time, a treasure among my most cherished memories, an image that can only be conveyed through words. And a little intimate secret: her toenails were painted red.

She was a fucking neck-breaker machine, intergalactic! Stratospheric!

I didn't say a word, but with my gaze, I told her everything. The silence was almost as imposing as she was. When I was about to get up from the bed, she gestured with her hand for me to wait. She sat down beside me, rested one foot on the bed, and slid a stocking over it. She repeated the same movement with her other foot. In that moment, it was as if the world around her ceased to exist—she seemed to be in an empty cathedral or under a starry sky, where silence feels immense, almost infinite.

She then proceeded to put on her boots.

Once she was finished, we both stood up suddenly. I stepped ahead to open the door for her. She grabbed her handbag, and with our hands intertwined after closing the door, we set off to conquer the night.

Our shadows against the nineteenth-century brick buildings suddenly blended with the colourful street murals. It was almost offensive that no one was admiring us from the wrought-iron balconies of the Victorian-style row houses. Tree-lined streets, bicycles leaning against posts, and a few drunkards disrupted our perfect landscape.

A little street library caught her attention, and among the abandoned books, she adopted a humble French-English dictionary bound in black leather. "Je pense, donc je suis," I said without thinking.

Around the corner, a line of people revealed the location of the first bar we'd hit. It looked lively from the outside; the stupid social proof pulled us in. People were constantly entering, showing their IDs. When it was our turn, a tall bouncer with masculine features and a flattened nose approached us. Though I stood right in front of him, he ignored me completely, turning to her instead. "Hey, love, I had that exact same dictionary once," the brute said with a strong West Sydney accent. She looked at him and responded in a cool tone, "That's nice."

As the mancancan prepared to fire his second shot, I made my presence known. "Est-ce que tu parles français, connard?" I used the informal structure with deliberate sarcasm. The so-called master of social interactions replied with a simple, "What?"

Fuelled by an excess of dopamine and cortisol in my blood, I turned to her and said, "Este es un imbécil." She laughed, and we showed our IDs before stepping inside. He might have been much taller than me and looked intimidating, but I had grown up in Bogotá.

Already inside, the music pulsed through the dim, crowded space.

Unbearably sexy from head to toe, she danced with punctilious care, balancing on the edge of sobriety and deliberation, always mindful not to raise her arms too high, lest her dress reveal what could spark a tidal wave in the eyes of one—or many—attentive observers. One of those attentive observers was me, making my way towards her with two vodka-Red Bulls in my hands.

The party's atmosphere buzzed—a vibrant mix of electronic pop, hints of dance, LGBTQ anthems at just the right moments, nostalgic hits, and a few contemporary crowd-pleasers. A drag queen, serving as the master of ceremonies, punctuated the sets with charismatic, spicy interjections. It was good, but it wasn't quite what we were looking for.

On the second round of drinks, we ordered Fireball shots, which we downed in one go, maintaining unbroken eye contact—a silent gesture of respect.

Casually, while we were giving everything on the dance floor, a tanned, athletic man approached her and, without much shame, said he just wanted to congratulate her on having such a sexy boyfriend. After giving me a once-over and offering her a polite goodbye, he disappeared into the sea of lights and motion.

She turned to me with a teasing smile on her lips. "You're wasting your time with me," she joked. "You should follow that confident guy in the tight pants."

The constant rhythm changes had worn us out, and sealing our departure with another shot of cinnamon whisky, we threw ourselves back into the night—but not before I showed my good manners, turning to the bilingual bouncer with a casual, "Bonne soirée, mon ami."

The bustle of conversations, the clinking of glasses, and the hum of light traffic served as our guide to escape a labyrinth of narrow streets. A long main road greeted us with clusters of people around fast food shops and bars. We weaved through the crowd while our blurred reflections in the large shopfront panes watched us with frustration, unable to follow. With no clear direction, the magnetic needle of memory led us to an underground nightclub—a place where a past version of me had once lingered.

A cadenced and hypnotic rhythm—one that deserved to be sent into space on a NASA spacecraft, to be played continuously and endlessly so its sound waves could envelop the entire universe, poured from the descending stairs of the bar we were about to enter. Two minutes in line, ten seconds getting our IDs checked, twelve seconds paying for the cover charge, and there we were, descending illuminated steps bathed in vulgar red light. Morbid shadows leaning against the railings, remnants of other tales of enchantment, perfectly complemented the atmosphere we had both been searching for. Inside, a dark room stretched before our intertwined hands where only the DJ booth, glowing under a bluish light, and a bar on the opposite side—where two figures moved swiftly under a faint white glow—stood out in the dim haze. Between them was a mass of souls dancing in front of the DJ booth, while smaller groups swayed with less exuberance in the corners. Occasionally, a light tried to sync with the melody that condensed this hole of brilliant pleasures, but it always fell behind.

Our bodies swam through the sweaty crowd and a myriad of dilated pupils until we finally reached the bar. A thin man whose face seemed to scream he wanted to die served us with unimaginable speed.

Without my uttering a word, he read the future movements of my lips. Two plastic cups. The ice scoop stabbed the bin twice, dropping four cubes into each cup. With his right hand, he poured vodka into a jigger and swiftly tossed it into the first cup before repeating the motion for the second. Simultaneously, he slid a card reader towards me with his left hand. As the inaudible click reached his eardrums, he poured Red Bull into both cups, filling them to the brim. All of this happened while he was already serving someone behind me. I didn't applaud him—not because I didn't want to, but because my hands were too busy holding the cups he'd handed me before I even noticed.

Little by little, we submerged ourselves in the waves of the rich and complex nuances of textured music. The arms of strangers floated like spectres among the dim, flickering lights. Our faces separated by only a few centimetres moved in harmony, her right hand swaying in the air while her left, at thigh level, held both her drink and her dress. My shoulders followed the rhythm of the pleasure glimmering on her face, a miraculous synchronicity broken only by sips of an energetic sweetness and slight sharpness with an effervescent finish—not precisely coming from our glasses, but from our warm mouths.

We were trapped in a loop in which every layer spun by the DJ's touch pushed us closer to that precarious edge between self-control and uninhibitedness. A riser that seemed like a lifeline was merely a mirage, heightening the anticipation. Our eyes closed, our minds lost in the fucking void, and the drop, like the gravity of a thousand suns, pulled us back into our bodies, igniting a chain reaction of movement that spread from the roots of our veins and arteries to the last hand in the air within the crowd.

Without, lamentably, even a particle of methylenedioxymethamphetamine coursing through our neurotransmitters, the high was astonishingly pure. Despite the variety of blinking eyes scattered around us, privacy reigned, fostering our complicity. Without any purpose, yet desiring everything, I leaned closer to her neck, inhaling her scent—a morbidly alluring, intoxicating aroma that filled my lungs and, alchemically, transformed into words as I exhaled—words brimming with the rawest, most carnal vice: Lustful! Impetuous!

"You are so fucking sexy, mamasita."

The vowels rolled out, clearer and fuller, each syllable stretched and emphasised as if echoing across the vast expanse of the Andes.

With her eyes closed, her raised jaw revealed the graceful curve of her slender neck, speckled green lights scattered across her skin, forming iridescent scales. Her sinuous movements paralysed me; she wasn't Eve—yet I felt the invitation to the forbidden. Slowly descending from the music, her eyes opened and locked onto mine—an ophidian gaze, cold and impenetrable.

I was ensnared in her mystique. Her plastic cup slipped from her fingers, bouncing on the floor four times as her hands found my neck, pulling me into her world. Without stopping her dance, she kissed me. She conducted the orchestra with her reptilian tongue.

Venom in my throat.

In response, my hands slid to her waist, drawing her closer, intertwining her legs with mine. Despite the thick denim of my jeans and her thin underwear, I felt the humid heat of hell on my thigh. Red lights filled the air, like embers from a phoenix's tail—sparks of memory reigniting, blazing back to life in that instant.

Our lips parted, leaving viscous particles adrift in the air. She turned her neck first, followed by her shoulders, and the braid of her hair shamelessly brushed against my chest. Though not made of ferromagnetic material, her ass, carrying a north magnetic pole, was drawn irresistibly to the south magnetic pole of my belt buckle. My pelvis and thighs bore the weight of her dance, while the edges of my nails traced the curves of her figure in slow, deliberate movements from top to bottom. I playfully bit the lobe of her left ear, the universe, condensed in our loins.

Some might recount that she took my hand and pulled me out of the crowd; others might firmly argue that I was the one guiding her, zig-zagging between silhouettes. Some will say I teasingly pushed her into the bathroom, and she was the one who smiled as she shut the door. Others will claim she entered first, and I knocked—only for her arm to pull me in, leaving nothing but the scent of my cologne in the air as the door slammed shut. Not all of them were wrong. We were one being in that moment, a mythological beast with four legs, four arms, and a single heart.

In that cubicle, there was a "clean" toilet sitting at the back, walls covered in stickers, and a metal sink with only one knob. Above it, a bluish light cast an eerie glow over the inevitable mirror where countless faces had paused, searching for approval and self-deception before plunging back into the fray—and let's not forget the bin for discarding syringes tucked in a corner. Clearly, we'd found the crème de la crème of the city's party scene.

A slight misalignment from the bathroom's last renovation—exactly five months and twenty-four days ago—had left an almost imperceptible gap. Through it, voyeuristic sound waves slipped, bearing silent witness to her hands sliding deliriously under the back of my shirt. Her face expressed a mystical rapture, while my lips hungrily melded with the skin of her neck. My hands, without restraint, squeezed her ass so hard that my fingerprints marked her pale skin.

We were the omen of what would unfold 4.5 billion years from now, when our galaxy collides with Andromeda. A single giant elliptical galaxy will emerge—"cleverly" nicknamed "Milkomeda" by "experts"—birthing new stars, extinguishing others. In this moment, we were a microcosm of the universe's evolution: chaotic, yet inevitable, beautiful yet destructive.

Each of our actions in that moment added a letter to the story that was unfolding between us, just as the weight of my fingers now falls carefully on the keyboard, forming letters that capture my most vivid and ardent memories—words like those I whispered into her delicate ears. My salacious tongue traced from the helix to the tragus, while her hands moved away from my back to climb up to my defined chest, feeling the wild rhythm of my heartbeat. She pushed me slightly into a void, only to pull me back, silently demanding space—a space that was soon saturated with voluptuous desire when those same hands, which had momentarily restrained my animal instinct, descended to my belt, unbuckling it with reckless precision.

Thirsty and subdued, my right hand breached the personal space of her face, my thumb tracing the contours of her lips as if a blind man reading with the most profane concentration, until I slid it into her moist mouth. An infinite suction of pleasure presaged acts my fingers dared not write.

FUCK!

My gaze floated in the vastness, caught in whirlpools of carnal delight, only to slowly descend and be captured by hers. She was my prison; I was hers—her prisoner, her slave—but it wasn't enough for me.

My right hand gripped her neck as I leaned in, her open mouth receiving mine like a sacred sacrament.

Labios humeantes e insaciables.

Slowly, she straightened against the wall.

It was my turn—she knew it. I turned her around; her hands pressed against the wall, pushing slightly as her hair tangled in my kisses. My tongue traced her shoulders as my knees lowered me to her waist, where her ass peeked out like a waning gibbous moon turned ninety degrees. My hands transformed it into a full moon as she pushed back slightly, forming a feline curve in her spine.

My index finger tugged and shifted the barrier that protected what was most sacred. My face plunged into her damp flesh, and my tongue recited the most infamous verses. The dam burst, and her voice, like a bell, triggered my Pavlovian instinct. In one motion, I was back at her level. A playful tease, suspense, my hand firmly grasping her braid.

Juices mixed.

Mixed into rhythm.

Rhythm into madness.

Slowly, deeper.

Her thirsty flesh, little by little, I delved further into the depths. Gasps, ragged breaths, obscene words, moans, energy, rhythm. My left hand on her breasts, one of her hands conspiratorially pressing against my abdomen, urging me to slow down.

I didn't obey, increasing the intensity.

A gentle knock on the door interrupted us. We ignored it for 238 seconds. Our reflections in the mirror were laughing at the audacity of our indulgence. I adjusted myself to conceal the unconcealable, and she masterfully straightened her dress.

In what world is it more decent to pretend to consume clandestine drugs than to celebrate love?

We opened the door, and the music hit us like a wave. Two bouncers guided us towards the exit. We walked out proudly, heads held high. The night was still breathing. Our hands intertwined, our steps buoyed by laughter.

It must have been around 1 a.m., or perhaps I am just misremembering—or to be exact, it was 1:33 a.m. The night was warm. We didn't bring up what had just happened; it was something normal in our past. The norm was not to get caught. We walked for about seven minutes until a striking Irish pub lit up our path. The bouncer, a man around 60 years old with a friendly demeanour but with a few ghosts lurking in his eyes, winked at us and, without asking for our IDs, let us in.

The place had a timeless charm, its dark wooden facade evoking visions of cobblestone streets in Dublin or Galway—streets where Gabriel Conroy probably had heard the snow falling faintly through the universe. Inside, the warm glow of light reflecting off beer glasses and steins immediately invited us to seek something refreshing. A poor choice on my part: "Can we get two Jack-and-Cokes?" clumsily escaped my mouth. I should have asked for a Guinness or a Jameson, but, then again, consistency wasn't one of our virtues that night (later on she ordered some rum with apple juice)—nor, it seemed, of the pub itself. From the speakers, the unmistakable voices of the Starchild and the Spaceman echoed, singing "do do do do do do"

"Thump-thump-thump," my voice mimicked the beat of the drums. The clean, rhythmic guitar combined with the deep, infectious groove of the bass wrapped around us as we searched for a place to sit.

Stanley's sensual voice blended with mine: "Tonight… darkness"

The song transported me back to a distant memory, when I was barely twelve or thirteen years old, tasked, along with a few schoolmates, with finding an English song and perform it in front of the class. Our choice was this anthem by the New York band. Each of us embodied a member of KISS, complete with their iconic make-up. One of my comrades, whose features seemed more suited to the Shire than the stage, unintentionally ended up looking more like "Ratboy" than Catman. After days of rehearsing, we delivered three minutes and fifty-one seconds of badly pronounced English—a poor pronunciation that had followed me all the way to that pub table twenty-two years later.

She burst into laughter at my pantomime of the sample sound mimicking a whip crack: "whoosh-crack." From a nearby table, an old drunkard, drawn by my musical antics, stumbled over and invited himself to join us. Without waiting for our approval, he added his own poorly executed performance to the mix, a rendition more pitiful than mine.

When the song ended, the cheeky bastard lingered for a moment, clearly torn between wanting to stay at our table and realising he wasn't particularly welcome. Perhaps it was the intensity of her laughter or my shift into Spanish as I spoke to her, but he eventually shuffled back to his corner, singing the next song.

I dare say I remember every song that played that night, the precise order, what drink we were holding for each one, the exact words we exchanged, the number of times her eyes blinked, the number of times I went to the bathroom, and the blurry handsome stranger in the mirror who always nodded in approval. The kisses that filled the silences, how our fingers played mischievous games of their own, the moment we were told we had to leave, and the two sips it took her to finish her rum with apple juice, followed by the three sips that nearly had me throwing up in the bathroom. How we said goodbye to the bouncer, how we wandered through streets teeming with drunk souls after the Saturnalia, the homeless sleeping under newspapers and sheets in a corner. The two of us running hand in hand, daring the speed of a car horn, its lights catching the tips of her beautiful hair, freed from her braid. How we walked past where "mon ami" was still standing sentinel at the door of our first drinks. How we entered the hotel through the back door, the dark hallway illuminated by her phone's flashlight, pointing at the doorknob as she struggled to fit the key, both of us laughing at how uncoordinated we were. How Bushwick welcomed us back. Us, kissing ferociously but mocking the coordination we lacked moments before. Me taking off my shirt, her telling me she needed to go to the bathroom. Me lying on the bed, staring at the fan blades. Her returning and saying, "I killed my phone," the screen shattered from a minor fall. How we both erupted into uncontrollable laughter. Both of us rolling across the bed. The light stood witness as I held her face and told her, "You are the love of my life," her silencing my words with her kisses. Her warmth. My skin. Her face in my breath. How my lips traced the delicate curve of her ankles, or perhaps her ankles brushed my lips. The sheer cliché-joy of being alive. Complete surrender. Absolute cliché-abandon. A cliché-wave that engulfed everything. Time unravelled. Desperate kisses. Both of us collapsing under the weight of exhaustion. Her head—cliché-style—resting on my chest. Me inhaling the scent of her hair as my eyelids shut out everything—leaving only the infinite nothingness."

V

"The glow of a blazar billions of light-years away from Bushwick pierced my closed eyelids the next morning. I couldn't keep falling into clichés, and the intrusive interstellar light woke me up. She was still sleeping on my chest, so I carefully slid away to get up and close the curtains. I glanced at my phone, lying timidly on the floor, its battery drained. Rummaging through my bag, I found a charger, and as soon as my faithful companion reached 1%, it hysterically screamed in my face that it was 10:33 a.m. Our check-out from this makeshift hideout was at 11 a.m.

She looked so at ease in the tangled sheets. I gently shook her, and within the depths of her mind, she saw how the purple sky of her dreams began to blend immiscibly with green seas as she stopped flying, soaring through scarlet clouds. Out of nowhere, a quake of sound waves began to echo in the background: "amor, amor, amor." Then, at the horizon, the sky and sea collided, she shut her eyes tight, then opened them slowly. Her retinas captured a blurred silhouette, bathed in faint rays of light: it was me, standing with a glass of water, ready to soothe her parched throat.

"Mamasita, we need to get ready to go," I said. The words took form in her mind, and with her eyes still shut and eyebrows raised, she simply mumbled, "What the fuck." Returning to reality is brutal—a single droplet echoing through the grey matter, dragging the weight of the previous night. A monotonous drip that makes the external world unbearable. Her dry mouth accepted my offering as she propped herself up on her elbows and sat up on the bed.

This may sound like fiction, but by 10:54 a.m., we were both ready, with no trace of sensitivity in our eyes, stomachs, or moral compasses. The world had adjusted its contrast, and the fragmented, disordered flashes of the previous night took shape, leaving no room for uncertainty. With great finesse, she slid the room key into a safety-deposit box at 10:59 a.m., narrowly escaping a late check-out fee. The sun that morning seemed a little shy and hesitant, as if it had questions for us—questions the moon from the night before had refused to answer out of modesty.

Our first stop was a café. She ordered an oat-milk latte, I opted for a cappuccino. Her scrambled tofu arrived with quiet elegance, while my banana bread—served with a dollop of ice-cream—felt indulgent, even triumphant. It was the perfect formula to recharge: a fleeting luxury before the raw chaos of the festival. Our olfactory receptors savoured this last supper, immersed in the rich blend of coffee and breakfast aromas. Soon after that, the café's earthy fragrance acted as a neutraliser, resetting our senses in preparation for the crucifixion amidst the thrumming crowd of perspiring metalheads.

We were running a little late, so we grabbed an Uber to Randwick. I'd forgotten to mention that we'd be joined by one of my lifelong best friends—charismatic, eccentric, and loyal—and his partner, who were kindly waiting for us to set off together. Fortunately, the traffic that Saturday morning was light, and in no time, we were at my friend's apartment.

There's no point in detailing every moment—the warm camaraderie in the flat and the journey to the festival, the bands giving their all on stage, the crowd jumping in unison, the vocalist with "attitude" hurling insults at the audience while we cheered in celebration, canned cocktails in hand, the two of us spinning on the "Hurricane"—she screaming euphorically, I stoically praying for my life, our gums were coated with dirt and dust after diving into the mosh pit, the countless kisses we shared amidst waves of flying hair, sweat, and euphoria when the guitar shattered the massive stage speaker to announce that song. The song that has accompanied you through good, bad, and indifferent moments. The one that played while you went to the job you love—or hate, while you studied, during long and short showers. The one you first heard long ago, maybe recommended by a friend or on the radio. The one you've played over and over, whose lyrics your mind has rewritten, the one you've both loved and hated. The song you've imagined yourself performing in front of someone as jubilant as you are now, standing in awe of the music, the band, the genre that has given you a part of your identity. That musical piece that feels like it belongs to you alone, yet is shared—just for this moment—with a crowd of strangers in an ephemeral but universal communion. And when it ends, all you can say is, "¡Qué gonorrea de canción!"

An unforgettable evening—a magnificent tapestry of noise, sweat, and unrestrained joy. But as the final band prepared to take the stage, the heavens opened, and a downpour crashed over the festival. The fury of God lashed the crowd, and organisers, reluctantly defeated, called for an evacuation. We were urged to leave as quickly as possible.

The blasphemous flock had been punished.

Yet even in that chaos, we stayed close—united like Sodom and Gomorrah under Proust's pen. Her boots and my sneakers sloshed through rainwater as we paraded through the ecstatic crowd. The rain felt like both a curtain call and an encore—a fittingly wild ending to a day that would live forever in our memories. Of course we didn't look back as we left, avoiding even the faintest chance of being turned into beautiful salt statues.

Back in my comrade's lair, barefoot, drying off our damp skin and dressed in dry, sin-free clothes, we toyed with the idea of heading out to a local pub to continue the night. But the relentless weather and the thought that the next day we'd be heading to Wollongong for our skydiving adventure were enough to extinguish the small flames of illogical temptation.

After a lighthearted recap of the day — laughter, teasing, anecdotes from the past, and new tidbits about our lives — previously shared through social media, texts, and calls — that now demanded presence; it became a moment of connection. They knew about the existence of my ex-enemiga, and she had heard a bit about them. The evening naturally turned into an informal introduction, solidifying those impressions with ease.

That night, we stayed in my friend's living room, which had been thoughtfully prepared to provide us with great comfort: an air mattress, cosy pillows, clean sheets and blankets. After a drawn-out goodbye and the constant reassurance of "if you need anything, just let us know," our hosts retreated to their room, leaving her and me bathed in the silvery light of the night filtering through a window that opened onto a terrace.

The darkness outside sang softly through the steady rain. My arm served as a pillow for her head, a warm kiss, our legs intertwined, my right hand tracing the length of her back and hips, her breathing growing softer. My lips brushed against her brow. The day's accumulated exhaustion hung heavy on each eyelash. My mind quietly hummed: "All I ever needed is here in my arms…"

What an implausible morning greeted us the next day. The relentless deluge had battered the night, but as Earth turned to embrace the majestic sun, a gang of mischievous cumulonimbus and rogue nimbostratus fled the scene, leaving behind an incomprehensible and infinite blue. The ozone seemed perceptible just by gazing at the tiny mirrors of water pooling on the empty streets. Droplets clung for their lives to the tips of green leaves, catching the sun's warm glow and reflecting the landscape. As they fell, other droplets—still suspended in the air—were seduced by the sun's rays, and without resistance, allowed themselves to be pierced at just the right angle, leaving behind a fleeting chromatic sigh.

During my first yawn of the morning, an invincible and metaphysical spectator—wearied by existence—slumped onto a sofa as metaphysical as he was. His hands energetically rummaged between the gaps in the cushions until his fingers found a remote control, as metaphysical as himself and his sofa. He aimed it at the mundane tableau of my morning and, without hesitation, pressed the Fast-Forward button.

My fingers, which had been languidly rubbing my eyes at a speed of thirty frames per second, became nothing more than streaks scratching at reality at four hundred frames per second. Jerky, fragmented movements, unnoticed small details—morning kisses, a glass of water, greetings to my hosts, a quick coffee, each of us taking turns in the shower. The otherworldly voyeur, though tasteful, couldn't resist slowing the speed as my beloved stepped into the shower—who could blame him? But then, once again, his finger hit FF: us leaving in my friend's car, heading to Wollongong, vehicles turning into streaks of colour in the background, the sky's grandeur bleeding into oblivion. The impatient omniscient spectator rested his head on his arm, propped up on the sofa, trying to push the speed even further, growing frustrated.

And then, in an instant, we were standing before an instructor explaining how to land. With a leap of excitement, the desperate, timeless observer pressed the Rewind button, then hit Play to savour this magnificent moment. My comrade, my beloved, and I were preparing to jump. My comrade's girlfriend, however, opted to stay behind, promising to film our landing, and declaring, "I'll never do that."

The sky stretched vast and clear, as if challenging us. The lazy deity leaned forward in his seat, the remote dangling loosely in his hand, a smile teasing the corners of his lips.

Showtime was just a button away.

It wasn't the first time I had done this. To celebrate one of my solitary birthdays, I had gifted myself a tandem jump. Back then, all my senses felt heightened, every moment sharper, as though I were experiencing life for the last time. It was an experience that redefined the word "fantastic". But this time, I was repeating that intense thrill with people who truly mattered to me. The tension grew with each passing second, bringing us closer to the sliding door of our airborne vessel. At the press of a red button, that door would open, releasing its living cargo from more than 15,000 feet above the ground.

I watched my friend slide his legs into the harness that would tether him to the professional jumper (he had done this before as well). My beloved, on the other hand, looked a bit nervous but, as always, carried herself with composure, masking her nerves. For me, it wasn't entirely second nature, but I needed to reinforce my confidence so as not to give her the wrong impression. Instructions on what would happen were given: "Lift your legs when landing like this." The instructor demonstrated in a comical position how we should hold our legs at a 90-degree angle to allow the tandem skydiver to land smoothly. Goggles hung around our necks, a flotation device was secured at our waists, and how could I forget the stylish parachuting pants we were given? After the rain from the previous night, the ground would be muddy. Que nivel, Maribel.

We boarded the bus that would take us to the airstrip where the plane awaited us. Silence filled the bus, broken only by the murmurs of the professionals. Tension soared to astronomical levels as AC/DC blared in the background. At the airport, we entered a waiting-room. Eight souls, bound for the sky. My group of three looked confident, buoyed by a mix of courage and anticipation. Across from me sat two young men, perhaps in their early twenties, with sharp features and lean builds. Their black hair framed faces frozen in fear—they looked more nervous than a heavy man perched on a fragile plastic chair.

Two, three, four minutes passed before they opened another door. A short corridor, five steps, and a door leading to a field where the horizon perfectly separated the ground and the sky. The plane's engine was roaring at full power. The instructors gave us one last cheer, and then fifteen steps—no hesitation. There was no turning back. Right foot on the foothold, left arm pulling the body's weight. Fate closed its eyes and chose her to be the first to jump from the plane. I would be second, my friend fourth. The rest faded into insignificance.

One by one, like lambs to the altar: instructor, jumper, instructor, jumper—each pair vanished into the void, swallowed whole by the open door.

As we settled into position, with the door closing behind us, I reached for her hand. I kissed it gently, a fleeting touch meant to anchor us to something real amidst the chaos. She looked at me and smiled, her eyes holding a quiet strength, though a flicker of nerves still danced at their edges.

Hypothetically, as the plane began its journey down the runway, the sound of the engines, like the bullying antagonist of an American movie, dominated and subdued all the timid little sounds that dared to emerge around me. Yet with certainty, I could perceive a fine gallop accelerating like a dark mane flowing over the open plains—a "lup" produced by the closing of the atrioventricular valves. "Lup-lup," and in the midst of each "lup," a muffled hoof striking the field, "dup," produced by the closing of the semilunar valves. "Lup-dup, lup-dup," the systole and diastole cadence of my beloved's ventricles. "Lub-dub, lub-dub, lub-dub" turned into "lubdub-lubdub-lubdub."

Gradually, a soft breath intertwined with the accelerating rhythm, adding a subtle melody that lingered. The voice of my instructor cut through: "Ready, mate." The click of several harnesses anchored us to the runway. A red light paused the music—brief silence, a cardiac and respiratory arrest. A faint sigh at the back of the plane restarted the beat. The yellow light: imminence. Nothing more to say. We all moved our heads to the rhythm of our hearts. Obviously, we didn't, but it adds a touch of flair.

I need you to go.

Green light. The door slid open. The music was shoved out by the cold wind. My beloved and her guardian stood at the edge, her head tucked against the collarbone of the man who knew how to fall for a living, her chin pointed higher than I had ever seen it when she walked.

¡Jueputa!

The world swallowed her.

Wow.

We were separated, but my soul leaped with her—and God entered me. At the edge, I ignored the instruction to keep my chin up—I looked down, searching for her. It was only a second before I obeyed. I looked up at the sky, my instructor and I bound together in vertigo. Memorable. Gravity showing me its power, my anxiety peaking with the urge to be near her.

A moment for eternity.

Six hours later, the two of us walked along a beach, both in swimsuits, the sunset caressing tiny white crabs that scurried away from our footsteps. A man with rolled-up trousers and a fishing rod strolled by. We were unscathed, still talking about the experience, about how when she landed, I followed just seconds later, hastily unhooking myself from my protective harness to walk towards her. I kissed her ozone-filled lips, her face flushed, her voice trembling—a tremor that had vanished under the light of that beach. Above us, the sky was painted by angels, a vivid canvas to remind us that after brushing against infinity, everything becomes tinged with delirium, incomprehension, and a profound reverence for the gift of being alive.

That night, we stayed in a small town near Wollongong, a tiny place wrapped by bushland. By 7 p.m., not a soul was wandering the streets. Luckily, we stumbled upon a modest Italian restaurant, where we shared a few beers and limoncellos. We laughed at the videos of our jumps, wandering through the deserted streets afterward. Words were scarce; the dopamine crash from the day's adrenaline wore us down, seeping into our bodies with every passing moment. Eventually, we made the best decision: saying goodnight to our travel companions and retreating to our room as soon as we hit the hotel again. She was wearing white that evening—a detail I can't bring myself to leave out.

The faint glow of the sister of Eos and Helios streamed through a small window. Barely two minutes had passed before my mamasita was already asleep. The room was at the perfect temperature, and her head resting on the pillow seemed to demand that I surrender to rest as well. Without hesitation, I turned off the light and lay beside her, letting my entire being settle next to hers. The silver glow served as a blanket, a premonition? Selene had fallen in love with

Endymion, watching him sleep in a cave. I smiled at the thought—leaving the window open, would the Greek goddess abandon Endymion tonight, enamoured by my beloved? Would she forsake her eternal love for the chance at a sapphic infatuation? I was fucking tired that night, but somehow, I could still shoulder the weight of my own imagination.

The next day, we woke up very early. Our travel companions suggested visiting a nearby beach where we could see and interact with stingrays—a unique addition to our trip before heading back to Sydney. We took their advice and ventured there. Though the name of the beach escapes me, as does the count of rays brushing against my feet, I clearly remember bidding farewell to my great friend and his girlfriend upon arriving back in Sydney. From there, we boarded a train to a hotel my ex-enemiga had thoughtfully booked for us to spend two days before the arrival of the New Year."

VI

"The train ride was peaceful; both of us still somewhat tired, sharing a pair of headphones, our heads leaning against each other. We got off the train and headed to an area filled with tall buildings. After several minutes, we slid through an automatic glass door. She had reserved a room in what I could only describe as a proper hotel. I tried to hide my astonishment, but it lingered in the corners of my thoughts.

We ascended in an elevator to the reception area (yes, the reception required an elevator!), where she gestured for me to sit while she handled the check-in. My face, doing its best to mask both surprise and nerves, complied with a feigned nonchalance. Just two minutes later, she returned, signalling for me to follow. Back in the elevator, she pressed the button marked "29."

Madre de Dios, I thought.

It was the first time I'd ever slept so high above the ground.

We stepped out of the elevator into a long corridor. Ten steps. She pulled out a key card and unlocked the door. The last time I had opened a door with a card was in my home country—a day when my not-so-good habits had led me to slide my ID card along the edge of a door. The rigid plastic scraped against the wood as the card was inserted into the narrow gap between the frame and the door. Patience and desperation were key. The cold, stubborn latch offered resistance until I heard the click and felt a surge of relief.

This time, however, the process was effortless. With a mere tap of the key card against the reader, the door opened as if by magic. It was spectacular. Inside, we had our own private bathroom. Spotless. The bedroom was separate from the kitchen—we had a kitchen! A living room with a television—I hate television—large windows offering a panoramic view of the city, and a beautiful balcony. My humility spilled across the polished surfaces of that sophisticated room, and after a few moments of marvelling at what she had arranged for us, I confessed that it was the most luxurious place I had ever set foot in.

She laughed, hugged me, and kissed me. It was the first time I didn't have to share the bathroom with more than five motherfuckers since my life as an immigrant began.

Though it might sound comical, the time we spent in that hotel room condensed into something eternal within our souls, much like our naked bodies. It wasn't the most erotic show in the world, but I decided to cook gnocchi for my dear ex-enemiga. There I was, standing in front of the stove, completely naked, risking the chance that some boiling liquid in its supreme state of ebullition might leap onto my manhood. I moved with feline sensuality, every gesture and posture devoid of calculation, yet somehow seductively charged. She watched me cook while sipping rosé, her gaze lingering, soaked in playful amusement. It was, in its own peculiar way, a perfect dinner.

Stepping out onto the balcony afterward, we noticed a sign warning that the area was under 24-hour surveillance and that throwing anything off it could incur a fine—or even jail time. We were gonna throw our shyness. Naturally, this led to a mutual dare: "Bet you won't go out there naked and stay for X minutes." Naturally, neither of us could resist the challenge.

In unison, we slid open the glass door and stepped outside. It was no later than 5 p.m., and we were surrounded by hundreds of windows in nearby buildings, each one revealing a universe separate from ours. It was impossible to know if we brought satisfaction to any prying eyes nearby, if we became an anecdote for a dull conversation in a local pub, if our bodies were captured by a semi-professional cameraman—with an iPhone, or if a security guard used footage from the surveillance cameras to upload it onto some obscure adult site, satiating the voyeuristic appetite of someone in a corner of Slovakia, Yoknapatawpha, or Cómala.

As absurd as the thought may have been, it didn't matter. The time and privacy we shared in those nights—

and the golden hours that followed—were intensely pleasurable. Our souls, ravenous for connection, devoured every moment, yet our fragile, carnal bodies struggled to keep pace. If we had been made of wood, we would have burned that entire suburb to ash.

On 31 December, at 9:48 a.m., our bodies crossed the threshold from hotel sanctuary to the unforgiving street. The air buzzed with a strange, anticipatory energy. The temperature, a sweltering 34 degrees, made everything more uncomfortable, especially with our bags slung over our shoulders. The plan was to return to my comrade's house, where we would stay for one more night—from 1 to 2 January. Obviously, we wouldn't be sleeping on New Year's Eve; the night would stretch from one party to another, ending with a pub visit in the early hours of 1 January for a final beer.

We retraced our steps to the train station. Onboard, our heads rested against each other as we shared headphones, lazily scanning our surroundings. At 11:11 a.m., we arrived at my friend's house, dropped off our bags, exchanged a few polite words, and quickly decided to make ourselves scarce. We didn't want to overwhelm our hosts and figured our absence would make the midnight New Year's hugs more meaningful.

My beloved and I set out for a walk, nothing too unusual. We stopped at a costume shop to see what accessories might channel the right energy for welcoming the rebirth of the calendar. She bought red contact lenses that would give her a vampiric touch—eyes like embers reflecting her supernatural nature. I, on the other hand, searched for a black mesh shirt to exude a rebellious and edgy vibe. Unfortunately, I looked more like a Mardi Gras orgy rookie, so I decided against it. Even the rainbow, had it seen me, would've wept with laughter.

We strolled through Sydney's CBD, being nerds at heart, stopping at a bookstore where we picked up a few titles, including The Mysterious Correspondent by Proust—a perfect match for my almost-mesh-shirt aesthetic. By 3 p.m., still without lunch, we opted for a rooftop bar where we sipped martinis. Prudence tugged at our collars after the third drink, reminding us the night would be long and moderation now would bring greater joy later. Without further ado, we returned to our friend's lair, where we transformed ourselves to be worthy of the dawn.

Photo check.

Her: olive green dress, boots, and her fabulous presence—nothing more to add. In a word: perfect.

Me: Black jeans, a cutoff shirt, and a red cap—imperfect but with swag.

Our party companions? Regal.

Being locals, they needed to make a few stops to wish friends a Happy New Year. Their first destination was a house party on Oxford Street. Thankfully, I didn't buy the mesh shirt. On the way, we stopped at a kebab shop, where she and I shared a falafel kebab—enough for both of us. At the first stop, we had a few beers, smoked a bit, and engaged in neutral conversations. In the bathroom, my mamasita slipped in her red contacts, which added a mystical touch—though they had to come out within an hour due to discomfort. Hugs and Happy New Year wishes flowed among strangers. I took a photo of her with Sydney in the background. Painful to describe—melancholy drowning my fingers. Again.

By 10 p.m., it was time to head to our party featuring a famous and "exclusive" English DJ whose résumé included baptisms, funerals, Ibiza crazy parties, YouTube videos, barbecue joint openings, bachelorette and bachelor parties, and weddings. We were in the best of spirits, carrying a secret tucked away in a few capsules—capable of turning even the most mediocre party into something extraordinary.

We stood in a tedious line for about thirty minutes to enter the nightclub, surrounded by streams of humanity. Voices floated through the air, forming eerie new galaxies. Some eyes were fixed on the entrance, while others flitted uncertainly from face to face. A space ahead, a step closer, shortening the distance to the security checkpoint where a photo would be taken, and the bouncer would check our

IDs to verify that the person on the card matched the one standing before them.

By 10:46 p.m., we were inside. The place was packed, people dancing wildly in every direction. We made our way to one of the multiple bars and ordered rum with soda—two tall glasses. Before long, we were back at the bar for a second round. I took my ex-enemiga's hand and led her to the bathroom. There was a line—how tedious—but the monotony was about to end. She entered one of the stalls first—we couldn't enter together since bouncers monitored everything. As soon as she stepped out, I took her place in the stall, locked the door behind me, and slipped my hand into my pants.

When I pulled it out, a bag with five MDMA pills and a "parachute"—a twist of powdered ecstasy wrapped in rolling paper—rested in my palm like tiny keys to Eros' playground. I quickly popped one pill into my mouth, swallowing it with a grin to myself. After stashing the magical bag back in its sacred spot, I put another pill on my tongue without hesitation.

When I left the bathroom, she was leaning against the wall, waiting. Without a word, I grabbed her by the waist and kissed her. My impish tongue passed the methylenedioxymethamphetamine to hers. Our eyes met in complicity; I saw her swallow the pill. Hand in hand, we returned to the bar and quickly ordered another rum-and-soda. The party had begun, baby.

Gradually, we made our way to the centre of the dance floor, everything around us accelerating as if Sagittarius A* were pulling us in. The music pounded, but anxiety painted our faces as we waited for the serotonin, dopamine, and norepinephrine rush that would soon manifest in dilated pupils, an uncontainable smile, heightened sensory perception, and uninhibited freedom. Sound waves floated around us, her body brushing against mine as she danced. We were in the dark heart of the galaxy, and every millimetre of my skin that felt her proximity ignited a new sun spinning at impossible speeds through my nervous system. My chest absorbed each beat, my arms yearned to detach and take flight.

She was everything.

Between blinks, her presence fused with the lights, timeless and infinite.

Suddenly, a voice sliced through the music: five minutes to midnight.

In those five minutes, I saw the first months with her, and the ones she wasn't there. Each memory plunged into Sagittarius A*, exploding into bursts of X-rays and radiation. Our bodies drew closer, her breath brushing against my collarbone. I whispered *"Te amo"*. She responded, *"I love you, Victor. I'm sorry for those months."* I cupped her neck, and with a slight nod of my head, I let her know no words were needed. My thumbs felt the tender wetness of a tear. We looked into each other's eyes. Her mouth parted slightly, mirroring mine.

Nine seconds to midnight.

Our mouths met, tongues locked in a fervent clash. She felt my tears streak down her lips. The year ended in that instant—a moment etched into eternity. Around us, strangers embraced their special someone, a friend, or simply anyone nearby. "Happy New Year" echoed on repeat, the music never stopped, but for me, the celebration felt singular, as if everyone were applauding us, that kiss. Even as our damp mouths parted and my dilated eyes opened, I swear I saw a cameraman in the corner wiping his own tears, moved by witnessing our most intimate moment in this ocean of glittering universes.

What a fucking immortal moment.

The avalanche of joy separated me from her, dragging me towards my friend to wish him a Happy New Year. I felt my toes touch water, forming ripples of sound—dark magic weaving through the floor.

The release of vasopressin granted us the superpower to consume endless liquids and keep dancing nonstop. The bruxism I felt was reflected in everyone around me, a collective grinding of teeth. Was it a mirage, or was I deceiving myself into believing everyone was equally empathogenically stimulated?

For a moment, I got trapped in the cadence of the beat, closing my eyes and letting my mind loop through vibrations of colours, a kaleidoscope of emotions. I was lost, and I didn't want to be saved. When I opened my eyes, there she was, possessed by the music, her body inebriated by the rhythm, moving with an ethereal grace. I shut my eyes again, and suddenly I was the one consumed. We were only 80 centimetres apart, yet with each blink, the distance seemed to shrink, an electrifying magnetism drawing me closer to her charged skin. I was at the peak of neurotoxicity—a magnificent, overwhelming effect. It felt too immense, too immaculate, for me to deserve it.

As soon as I felt her presence fully envelop me, I reached out and grabbed her by the waist, pulling her to me. She turned to face me, and my hand slid to her sacrum, pressing her closer. I inhaled the scent of her neck—it was pure cocaine, atavistic energy coursing through me. Licentious words slipped from my lips and danced into her ears, igniting an unseen spark between us.

The music erupted, shaking the floor, and we threw our arms into the air. Around us, a chorus of voices echoed in unison with the rhythm, chanting "uuuuu"—a hymn to the universe. For a moment, we were no longer individuals, but particles in a cosmic explosion, orbiting each other in this shared moment of ecstasy.

Predictably, the descent from euphoria began to soften our movements. The cascade of minutes in nirvana dwindled, and the monotony of reality crept closer. We still had four bullets tucked away in my underwear, but the reigning question loomed: was it worth using them at this party? It was around 3 a.m., with the current celebration set to end at 4, and the next one scheduled to begin shortly after, in a different location.

Without overthinking, still riding the wave of temporary neuroadaptation, we decided to leave the venue immediately, leaving behind one of the best moments of my life—that New Year's high—which I hope to remember not just today but in 20 years, should I make it to 54–is a memory to smile about, filled with melancholy, my face weathered by the traces of other moments—some less important, others perhaps more so—that would have etched themselves into my skin and shaped my perception of who I was, who I wasn't, and who I will be.

The warm night welcomed us and, with quiet insistence, urged us to embrace as we walked. It seemed to want to take a million photographs of us—flashes of starlight, their origins possibly long gone, touching our steps as if they were snapshots of something eternal.

What exuberance. As soon as we arrived at the venue, a massive crowd stretched along the queue—a collection of zombies from other parties. This early-morning event on 1 January was a magnet for characters like us, refusing to stop celebrating. Our bodies joined the great mass in waiting, some trying to outsmart others by cutting ahead.

Some attempted verbally with excuses like, "I was already up there," in a tone of defiance, or "My friends are up ahead" spoken with a hint of submission but physically asserting themselves, pushing forward with not-so-submissive hands.

We couldn't understand the delay in letting people into the venue. Then, suddenly, the crowd ahead began to part, and the sound of disgruntled screams cut through the air. Three bouncers, each towering over 1.95 metres and weighing 120 kilos, dragged a young man across the ground—a wiry figure, no more than 1.80 metres and 75 kilos. The scene unsettled many of us. What kind of place were we entering, where such brute force was casually deployed? Perhaps the frail man wasn't entirely innocent, but I had imagined the First-World would have more restraint. And yet no one, including us, interfered.

Shame on us.

My friend's girlfriend turned pale, visibly shaken by the spectacle. The clash between her lingering euphoria and that brutal moment compelled her to ask my comrade to leave. The combination of her unease and the fading remnants of the previous celebration proved too much. Their decision was swift, leaving us alone to face this relentless battle that awaited on the dance floor. A hug, a "Happy New Year," a "See you later at my place," and just like that, they exited the frame—no longer the protagonists of this chapter in our film.

Time dragged on, and the effects of the pills were further diluted in my bloodstream. My liver, like a tenacious crusader, worked tirelessly to cleanse the pagan toxins coursing through my veins, unaware of the surprise it would face in a few minutes. Finally, the crowd began to move. Svetlana, with her commanding aura, led the way, carving a path forward. The same process repeated itself: ID in hand, a photo to confirm we were who we claimed to be. Seven steps forward. A door to the right. Music spilled out like the voice of a possessed woman in the midst of an exorcism.

The door swung open, and we stepped into the chaos—a new round, baby.

The next act unfolded with an unspoken mission: the bathroom. An endless line of women waited for three stalls, while in the men's bathroom, there was only one stall and a urinal that could fit up to seven apes. As soon as I walked in, I moved with thunderous speed, cutting off a drunk guy to claim the stall. Like déjà vu, my hand slipped inside my underwear, fingers brushing against the small bag of pills. I swallowed one dry, stashed two back in the bag, and kept a third in my palm, tucking the magic pouch back into the warmth of my gonads before stepping out.

When I emerged, she was still waiting in line. Acting on pure instinct, I popped the pill into my mouth and, with reckless audacity, pushed my way through the women standing between us. Her wide eyes couldn't comprehend my impulse. Without letting her speak, I kissed her, slipping the magic between her lips. In that moment, I felt like Eve, and she was Adam—except this wasn't the Fall, this was Ascension. In my mind, I imagined her in an internal monologue:

"Augmented, open eyes, new hopes, new joys. Taste so divine, that what sweet before Hath touched my sense"

Translate to: "This is fucking hot."

I waited exactly 15 minutes before she was finally freed. By then, the pill had already taken flight inside me, and I could tell it had in her too. The way her skin brushed against mine sent a whirlwind of sensations through my entire body. Without effort, we jumped to the beat, losing ourselves deeper into the crowd. When I snapped back to awareness, our bodies were completely unhinged, moving with feverish abandon. The DJ was brutally good. Each drop felt divine, holy even.

Fatigue had become a myth.

I couldn't continue describing what happened next without first highlighting a defining feature of the venue where we were annihilating the dance floor. The façade was entirely made of glass, letting in the lights from outside and offering a view of one of Sydney's most distinctive landscapes. We were on the third floor, and the glass ceiling above us revealed the sky, painted in hues of purple and red, signalling that the Patron was about to arrive.

At 5:46 a.m., the sun took centre stage, merging with the music. Like the god it is, it shattered all false idols of glass, tungsten, halogen gases, and steel in a single, obliterating blow. Every single one of us in that glass temple was swallowed by the light. I felt its kiss on my right cheek, magnified ten thousand times over—pure fullness. I knew I wasn't alone in this unshakable devotion. Uxorious, consumed. Worshippers to something we couldn't name.

We all, in unison, revealed our awe at the magnificence of this sunrise. I turned to look at her, and she shaped a single word, breathless, like a prayer: "Fuck."

I responded, grinning, "Que gonorrea."

With every passing second, the party wasn't something we attended—it was something that had invaded us, filled us completely.

We stepped out at 10:33 a.m. The party was supposed to end at midday, but for reasons beyond my memory at this moment, we decided to leave early. We were two souls gliding through the streets of Sydney's CBD. We stopped at a pub—one cold beer each. Her eyelids began to surrender, and the wisest decision was to head to my friend's house. But of course, my inner demon seduced me into stopping at a bottle-shop to buy a bottle of rum.

We still had some energy—or so I thought. We took a tram, both of us lost in our own minds, our thoughts occasionally interrupted only by external signals reminding us where to get off. When we arrived at my friend's place, they welcomed us, and without hesitation, I presented the tribute to our friendship.

YouTube playing Lavoe, Blades, Colon, Los Diablitos, Los Inquietos, Diomedes…

My beloved ex-enemiga poured herself a glass of rum, and her body surrendered. Her eyelashes, heavy as velvet curtains, drew the night closed. I don't know what time I fell asleep, but I do know that I woke up at 7 p.m., lying in the living room with her by my side. My friend's girlfriend, amused, held the empty bottle up to me—an unspoken testament that he and I had finished the potion.

Yet my body, the same one writing these words, bore not a single trace of hangover. This body that has never betrayed me, a privilege. A luxury.

That night, we ate pizza and recounted the events before going back to sleep.

2 January. How I wish I had known that nine months later, I'd be writing this. Maybe then I would have used my last hours in Sydney to elevate this story, to endow it with something more than just the mundane—packing bags, grabbing breakfast, my friend dropping us off at the airport.

A wait.

A flight.

Nothing remarkable, only the silence that foreshadowed something undefined—that thing that always lingers beyond the circumstance, beyond what is yet to come.

That night, back home, we said our goodbyes. She had to return to her life, to work on 3 January. So did I.

No taste of finality. No grand conclusion. No Montagues and Capulets. Our beautiful, delirious mini-vacation had come to an end. The colours drained away, replaced by shades of grey.

Now, relentless memories accompany me.

And how I envy that past self."

The corner of the screen marks 2:04 a.m. The light bothers me, and I notice fingerprints on the surface, distracting my gaze. Rather than rereading the text, I find myself remembering how I felt reading it for the first time. I don't know how many glasses of water I've had, but my mouth feels dry. My hand reaches for the glass, I take a small sip, and I lick my lips. I dislike doing this. I take a breath, and my mind fixes on an idea: that text was nothing more than a desperate attempt to give meaning to memories, to keep them from becoming grey anecdotes, left with no one to tell them. A feverish emotional impulse, squeezing out every last drop of a memory before it evaporated, embellishing the past, idealising it. And if something is clear to me now that wasn't when I first read it, it's that perhaps the most valuable part of what he wrote wasn't the frenzy but the silences within all that chaos. And what if that room, where my past self also lived after him, had been a bubble, one where all those memories took on colour, where I imagine he smiled after writing, or perhaps where his torn soul howled? Where his everyday life was interrupted by the idea of immortalising himself, of seeing his life in another light. Where my new everyday life had crashed against that sublime self-indulgence, that literary exhibitionism filled with hedonistic vitality tinged with melancholy, Eros and Thanatos in an urban key, the intensity of desire under the shadow of the ephemeral. But my past self didn't see that. He saw a dramatic yet comedic man who caught his attention. He read him with a raised eyebrow, wondering if there was more to the echo. That it might be interesting to dig a little deeper.

I didn't necessarily delve deeper into those days; I simply read parts of the text on the following nights.

During the days that accompanied those nights, I wandered through the city, exploring, looking for new possibilities. Yet, strangely, the previous inhabitant of my room began occupying more space in my mind. For no apparent reason, I kept returning to certain paragraphs—perhaps searching for clues, perhaps driven by the stars.

Ironically, I found myself in the section where he spoke of Gemini—my own zodiac sign—reaching its peak, and the waxing gibbous moon turning full. That moonlight not only revealed Victor's face, distorted by dependence, but also pulled forth a memory of my own birthday last year at that moment—4 June 2023 celebrating with friends.

And though it wasn't particularly remarkable at the time, I now recalled looking at the full moon that night, that same silver light striking my face, sinking into my memory, drifting aimlessly, lost among countless other moments, stripped of meaning—until reality made it stand out in the void, giving it wings to impose itself on my present and form a connection.

Once again, the immortal silver light reappeared.

Despite being young, I wasn't entirely naïve, and I followed the pattern. Eleven days before the end of Virgo's reign, which ended on 22 September, led me to September 11-the supposed date of his birthday.

Cronus (Saturn) retrograde in Pisces occurred between 17 June and 4 November, 2023, fitting neatly into the narrative but adding nothing particularly specific.

Finally, since Libra begins on 23 September, the 14th day of Libra would be 6 October—his ex-girlfriend's birthday.

This analysis didn't take me long, but it fuelled my idea that there was something more, that the theatrical man had structured his lyrical narrative with a certain precision.

I wouldn't go as far as calling it mathematical, but it did reinforce within me the feeling of fate and inevitability.

At that moment, I assumed—naively—that only I could have noticed this subtle chronology.

Moreover, I had confirmed that the name my housemate had given me matched the author of the text when his ex-enemiga had said, "Te amo, Victor," I felt a strange sense of complicity.

On top of that, the guy had lived in my room just a few weeks before I moved in. That made me think that he was probably still nearby, and so was his ex-girlfriend.

This thought fermented in my imagination, giving rise to scenarios where I ran into them on the street, where they looked at me, realising—just by the glint in my eyes—that I knew their secret.

In my mind, I had already constructed their faces. She had an exotic beauty, or at least what I had learned to recognise as such—her eyes, hovering between honey and brown, full lips, black voluminous hair, and a beauty mark on her chin.

But beyond just her features, it was the vibe she gave off in my imagination. I pictured her with that Mediterranean allure, the kind that lingers in warm, chaotic markets and sun-drenched coastlines.

My mind, fed by movies, filled in the blanks, painting her like a Spanish gitana or a castanet dancer—red ribbon in her hair, gold earrings, the intensity of her gaze cutting through the night, ready to read my palm.

It was a stereotype, I knew, but it was the only frame of reference I had.

And him? A bald guy with green eyes, thirty-four years old and Latin American features. I had no movie reference for him, but I imagined someone who looked like he had seen too much and kept most of it to himself.

Walking through the city, my imagination automatically ruled out people who didn't match these descriptions. Strangely enough, in those first few days, I didn't see a single soul who fit the profile I had created.

The climate was perfect that December—mild and fresh, ideal for wandering through the long, luminous days. Endless afternoons where the sea breeze from the Antarctic Ocean cooled the air, preventing the heat from becoming suffocating. At night, the temperature dropped, and the wind gained strength, crashing against the windows of my room.

At the time, it never crossed my mind that the text—clearly fiction—might not just be a distorted mirror of reality. That the melodramatic man had invented the story and its main character during the cold months before summer as a way to explore his imagination and transmute it into reality. That perhaps it was nothing more than a product of idle time.

No. They had to exist, and the text was a confession of absolute obsession. That idea gave weight to every step I took in those days. The solution was to keep reading, to pay more attention to the details. I imagined myself finding clues, each one bringing me closer to him, to her, to them.

My lack of purpose during those days was too easily seduced by the mystery.

That makes me laugh now as I glance again at the corner of the screen to check the time—2:07 a.m. In three minutes, I have travelled through time.

I feel my eyelids slowly dropping as the minute changes to 08. I hate the tingling in my jaw caused by that air of languor running through my body. I inhale deeply, and my mouth opens slowly. I feel the involuntary stretch spreading across my face and neck. I yawn, stretching my arms wide. The brief shiver follows immediately. I feel relief, but I don't want the drowsiness to take hold of me. I place both hands on the desk, pushing myself upright to regain my posture.

I see the water. I see the screen. I see myself reading the text in the past. I see the screen again.

I know I should get up and stretch my muscles if I want to keep reading.

Or should I just go to sleep?

I don't know if I'll return to the text tomorrow. Or maybe I will?

No, I definitely won't return to it later.

I stand up and feel the weight of not maintaining an active routine, of spending my time on sedentary activities. I still have energy; I just need to drink more water, go to the bathroom again, maybe eat something small, and come back.

Yes, that's what I will do.

I did just that, and as I settle into my chair, I think about how oddly funny, quietly melancholic, and slightly unsettling it is to refer to my past self in the third person. I feel a sense of pity—he didn't know himself at that moment, just as I now fail to grasp certain fragments of the self that make up who I am today.

It's complicated to consider that perhaps I am the antithesis of that thesis. And it's heartbreaking to think that I might already be the synthesis. That idea terrifies me. But a long time ago, I stopped feeling fear—because I think I understood that every solution is false, that every life is a failure… I don't want to drown in those thoughts. Though over time, I've come to enjoy my contradictions, this isn't the moment for that. The screen is off, and its glossy charcoal surface reflects my blinking. I touch the screen, and in an instant, the light swallows my reflection, replacing it automatically with black letters on a dark background. Perhaps that is the fate that befalls us all—to end up as words. Joys, sorrows, the infinite possibilities of a life condensed into sentences and paragraphs.

The soul is in the letters.

I smile to myself because I think it's a beautiful thought. Someone should read it.

I need to stop thinking and focus on what comes next.

2:21 a.m., I read on the screen.

Why am I reading this? Why do I keep coming back to it every now and then? What kind of shade has this cast over my life? Did my past self ever imagine that, twenty years later, I would still be reading this over and over? What's the point of reading it again next year, or even in a month? Will I even come back to it? I think no one else has read this. Or has someone? Maybe he sent it to someone else, but I don't think so. Though it wasn't written for me, I have been its only owner. In fact, I am the only one who knows more than what the text itself says. I am the only one who can bring the words into reality and reality into words. If I had never read this text, would I still be the person I am now? The answer is obvious—no. Anyway, I don't want to fall into that spiral of thoughts—not now. I'll just keep reading and finish it, as I always do, before going to rest, knowing that I will likely revisit it again in a few months. Because this is something that belongs to me alone. A story that only I know. A part of me, despite never having lived it myself.

VII

"The first time I heard about the Schmidt pain scale, my less-than-sharp hearing—and my tendency to make excessive connections—led me to think about how vicious society had become, so much so that it had established a parameter to measure how excruciating it was to exist in this beautiful system we are all caught in. Fortunately, the surname of a certain Adam hadn't been repurposed for that.

My ignorance led me to research this fascinating classification of pain through insect stings, created by the entomologist Justin O. Schmidt—the only entomologist I had ever known before was the one who created Dolores, qué casualidad.

Schmidt—who had nothing to do with capitalism but plenty to do with masochism—developed his scale based on personal experience, letting himself be stung by different hymenopterans. The scale runs from 1 to 4, with level one being the sting of a stingless bee (Trigona), and level four belonging to the bullet ant (Paraponera clavata), whose sting delivers a toxin called poneratoxin. A fitting name if it were whispered in a dark alley, right outside a bar where bad deals are made and worse ideas are born.

Without drifting too far, this substance is a neurotoxic peptide that affects sodium channels in nerve cells, inducing a pain often likened to being shot—which is why the bullet ant earned its name. I have never experienced a gunshot wound, but I did have a brush with a sharp metal once—during a street fight that left me with a scar and an anecdote rather than excruciating pain.

Schmidt describes the pain of a bullet ant sting as walking barefoot over burning embers with a rusty nail driven into your heel. The mere description is dreadful, but if I were given the option to feel the kiss of the little ant a few times instead of what I've been feeling these past months up until today, I would take it gladly. Emotional pain is shit, amigo. At least the bullet ant won't gaslight you. Alas, my brain—our brain—the brain, in all its complexity, doesn't fully distinguish between a physical wound and shattered attachment. Someone sitting on your chest, watching you suffocate, the throat tightening, not from crying, but from something lodged there, something unspoken and thick, the stomach caving in on itself—a psychosomatic abyss.

Fuck, it's not just drama, it's fucking biology.

But I won't get ahead of the story. The agonising cycle of comings and goings, of uncertainty, of viscous anxiety and gelatinous depression, will come later—just as it did in real life. My ex-enemiga and I had just returned from our little week in Sydney.

How difficult it is to approach what happened in the first days of this year from where I stand now. Despite those days being marked by intense sobriety, it feels as if my hippocampus had lost the ability to turn experiences into tangible memories—I was still intoxicated by the glorious emotions of our trip. I wouldn't say those days were forgotten, but rather that they were never truly stored in the first place.

And yet, one memory stands out in the darkness: my ex-enemiga and I were at a pub a few days after returning. It was an important day because, during the trip, we hadn't talked about what we were. But in my mind, she had been my girlfriend again from the moment I saw her on the bus to the airport.

Gin and tonic was the drink of choice for this crucial conversation. I don't remember how we got to the topic, but I do remember clearly that I asked her, "Do you want to be my girlfriend again?" Her answer was a yes. I took her yes and shaped it into a vow: "I will do everything in my power to make this fantastic. You won't regret making this decision."

For some reason, my imagination can't offer a more fitting backdrop to this moment.

My memory begins to rise, like Lazarus—not in four days, but in two weeks after that event. Not by a miracle of the Saviour, but by a date she had planned, a masterful plan: we would go to the mountains to explore them. To explore ourselves.

To be honest, I only found out where we were going on the morning of our date. The only recommendation I had received was to wear sportswear. The sole instruction: to be at a certain point at a certain time that Sunday morning in January.

The week had been tedious at work—though, to be fair, every week is tedious when you're doing something that doesn't ignite the deepest part of your soul. But food doesn't magically appear on the table, and dreams are built on effort and confrontation with monotony. For many, reality is simply the fulfilment of desires imposed by the images surrounding us, dictating what should be desired. For many others, it's bringing home sustenance to a house abandoned by the hands of God. And for many more, it's maintaining a vice that distances them from that same monotony. What a boring thing to think about. In the end, we all need a "why" to keep producing and, therefore, consuming.

It was 8 a.m. when I stepped out of my house. Fortunately, the meeting point was only an eight-minute walk from my door. The day was magnificent. The sun, rejuvenated after bathing in the depths of the seas—the poet winked at me—greeted me with a cheerful "Good morning, champ." A few timid clouds seemed to make a half-hearted attempt to veil the bare and shameless blue of the sky. The absence of traffic noise made my steps stain the tranquillity of the morning. In the distance, judgemental birds chirped, mocking the lightness in my stride, laughing at the unfiltered joy I carried in my walk.

Arriving at the port—by the way, the port was our meeting point, which led me to romanticise the idea that our date would involve something maritime. As usual, I was wrong—I spotted her silhouette in the distance, her hands resting on the railings. With stealth, I infiltrated her perimeter without her noticing: two steps to the right, a ballerina's leap to the left, a ninja's sprint, crouching low, I crept up behind her, my nose just ten centimetres from her eardrum. The wind, my ally, carried my breath in her direction. Some sixth sense made her turn slightly, just enough for her gaze to meet my eyelashes. I stole her breath for the briefest instant, but she barely flinched, her lips curving in amusement, like she had expected my antics all along.

At that moment, I felt like the clumsiest of "pisa suave"—a ghost in the jungle, invisible until the moment of attack, specialised agent from a certain Colombian guerrilla group. A popular saying claims that a pisa suave can easily eliminate eleven military targets in a single ambush, that they roam naked with a knife in the dead of night, blending with La Llorona and El Pate Tarro, "rezados" by brujos and possessing the precision to slit the throat of anyone unfortunate enough to cross their path. Some say they don't just vanish after the kill, they leave behind whispers, a final trick, an explosive *chao*. They are envied by every feline in the world, feared by the bravest soldiers, and, for the ultimate horror—some of them are not older than fourteen.

I take my eyes off the screen, my neck tilting back as I stare at the white, sterile ceiling. It feels so high, distant— detached. Maybe one day, what I'm writing now won't carry the velvety weight of melancholy. Maybe I'll read it with the eyes of someone who no longer aches at the memory. Or maybe it'll hurt even more. What does it matter? Maybe I won't even read it again. Maybe this moment will be relived and reimagined by someone else, inside their mind. Perhaps they'll see two figures dressed in dark sportswear, their shadows either chasing or escaping them, stretching towards the west-northwest, somewhere between 290 and 310 degrees azimuth—what precise imagination this reader has. Both boarding a bus: her, confident; me, surprised. The seats filled with people from every walk of life, their scattered conversations weaving into the dull hum of the engine. My lips brushing against her left cheek. Short dialogues, filtered and polished by the writer, now playing in the reader's mind — versions that have little to do with what was actually said. Even my face, reconstructed through the imagination of the bibliophile, wouldn't quite resemble the one I wore that day. And hers? No amount of imagination could do her beauty justice.

A jump in perspective — the bus now seen from above, an aerial shot, the view of a bird. It descends, flying at window level, almost kamikaze, glimpsing us inside. The two of us gazing out the left window, the reader at our side, watching as the blur of houses fades into the blur of green. The driver narrating the route as he carries us towards the mountain. My hand intertwining with hers. Her eyebrows raising, teasing at a surprise yet to come.

The bus slows, blending us into the crowd as we step off. Despite the altitude, the sky feels more distant. The wind wages war against her long hair, pulling it, twisting it, failing to free her from my grasp. Hands don't let go. A few steps forward, and a panoramic masterpiece unfurls before us — a clash of nature and civilization, rust-coloured rocks rising among faded greens. Mountains in the distance. And beyond what feels like an abyss but isn't, a river coils through the land. If you search for it, the port where we began is still there, saluting us from below. Countless rooftops blur into one indistinguishable canvas. A game of memory, or maybe just a game for one — finding one's home from above.

The air is crisp. The world, muted. A cocoon of stillness, of solitude shared.

Perhaps that's the image the reader conjures, were I to describe what I think I saw that day.

We felt flattered by the relentless battle between the icy wind and the stubborn rays of the sun—an arduous competition to kiss our faces. At that moment, neither was the winner, though the sweat on our foreheads after hours of hiking through the mountains eventually raised the hand of a clear victor.

We wandered up and down the trails, our conversations about playing the piano and owning a café in the future, embedding themselves into the rocks beneath our feet—paths forged by man, winding through nature.

From her backpack, the surprise: the most delicious burritos I've ever eaten, crafted by her own hands. Faint, dry streaks of sauce kissed the corners of my lips, my fingers perfumed with her seasoning. A mischievous smile—her mission had been flawless. She had never doubted it.

The two of us sat on the grass, trees blocking the horizon—possibly a void. Trees shielding our kisses from the eyes of the prying. Her warmth against me, our exhaustion making every movement slower, heavier, more deliberate.

Drained, we descended the mountain to its midpoint, stopping for a coffee at a roadside café, conveniently placed by a bus stop.

Nine hours later, we were back at the port that had seen us off.

10/10. My rating. Eternal gratitude for that experience. And to think—I didn't even like nature. Until then.

I've pressed the "delete" key so many times trying to start this paragraph that I wish the letters on its surface would fade away until only the bare black plastic remained. The frustration of reaching the end of an idea, reading it, and feeling like it's absolute shit. The inability to process, to explain, or even just to tell how, after such high moments that felt like a constant, I suddenly found myself at the edge of an abyss—where, without realising it, I put my full body weight, trusting the ground beneath me, believing it was just a brief moment of rest before taking the next step forward. But there was no ground. Just absence. The hollow pit in my stomach. Arms flailing in vain, searching for something to grasp. A desperate, laughable attempt at flight. I looked back—an opalescent sky, indifferent, already saying goodbye. Looking forward—nothingness. Hoping it was just a sleep myoclonus, shattered into a thousand pieces. But then, the impact—hitting the ground, body crashing in full force, everything inside implodes. The morbid spectator, disappointed that my body didn't bounce. The surprise of standing up, realising I am unscathed. But now, the void I fell into is inside me. And it weighs. It weighs so damn much.

It's 5 September. In six days, it will be 35 years since I first felt the light pierce my delicate eyes, since I felt my mother's sweat-soaked skin, her pain and relief translated into delicate kisses—the purest love. I rested on her beating chest, a memory that doesn't exist, because in that moment, I was not yet the one writing this—I was the void just beginning to be filled by the world.

Somehow, writing about my ex-enemiga and our story has been cathartic; unloading that weight onto words releases it, frees me. I've even laughed at how absurd I sound; my last name should be changed to Ariza and hers to Daza.

El hecho de que alguien no te ame como tú quieras, no significa que no te ame con todo su ser... Gabriel wrote.

Birthdays are shit.

I would have loved to share that day with her. In fact, there was a plan for it. A plan not so different from the one we had in March this year.

Seventy-eight possibilities.

Twenty-two major arcana, fifty-six minor arcana.

A dusty purple curtain in the background, a table covered with a chequered cloth that could have easily been used in my grandmother's house. A man with hypnotic eyes, extravagant jewellery, an enigmatic tranquility etched in the wrinkles of his face. Incense seemingly seeping from his armpits. His hands splitting the deck into three piles. Across from him, My Destiny—dishevelled hair, whisky stains on his shirt—sitting anxiously in front of him, as if at a blackjack table, waiting for the first card.

Slowly, the tarot reader gathers the three piles and lays down a card:

The Lovers.

No explanation needed. Without knowing the rules, My Destiny requests a second card, to which the inexperienced but sharp clairvoyant complies.

Two of Cups—representing partnerships, unions, romantic or friendly relationships.

The gambler bursts into laughter, disrupting the mystical air of this carnival stall. Another drink, more bills on the table, and the question: what follows?

Again, the tarot reader, empathetic and keenly aware that he can extract more money, shuffles the deck—this time without splitting it into three. It's unnecessary.

Whatever comes up, whatever he says, the drunkard will believe it all.

Two cards hit the table.

Eight of Wands.

The Chariot.

"Move quickly. Progress. Travel," whispers the mystic.

Of course. We have to travel again, thought My Destiny.

And so, my beloved ex-enemiga and I decided to take another trip to Sydney for a week, taking advantage of the fact that a music festival and a concert were conveniently spaced seven days apart. To top it off, my great friend would be travelling to the Philippines with his partner, leaving his den empty for a few weeks—I was, naturally, the perfect person to house-sit.

Destiny had spoken.

It was so easy to obey.

Too easy.

What My drunkard Destiny didn't know—what his foggy memory failed to recall from that tarot session—was that he had requested a third round. And in that final draw, the tarot reader's ringed fingers had laid down.

Three of Cups.

Five of Cups.

The reader knew their meaning immediately.

So he did the only merciful thing.

He poured one last cup, though this one came from a bottle rather than a deck.

Because some truths are best left undiscovered.

It was, in truth, an incredibly pleasurable trip—a week in which her presence felt more real than ever. Attempting to recreate in words everything we lived through in those ten days would be a feat of madness. In short, if my last name were Slothrop, the city of Sydney would have vanished beneath the sublime, warlike avalanche that struck it.

There's a photo from the last night there—a moment I don't even remember. She's holding me, her face tired, my eyes closed against her chest. She took that picture after an obscene amount of gin and tonics, in a state of supreme intoxication. I can still hear her words, playing back in my head even now: "You cried a lot, and your crying made me cry too."

I know I spoke about the love one should have for one's mother, and I must have drowned in a melancholic haze so thick that she felt the need to protect me. Her tears became part of mine, sharing in that strange and fragile moment.

Incredibly, despite drinking much more than I did that night, she took care of me—she made sure I got home.

There is so much disorder in that memory that to give it structure in fiction would feel like an insult.

The next morning, after I vomited up my lack of commitment to sanity in the form of pizza-stained regret, we set off for the airport, returning to our cold city.

I have no real excuse for not recounting the rest of those days in detail, because, to my eyes, they were perfect. And I want them to remain sealed in the only place where she and I alone possess them. Where—puta vida—they will stay untouched until our last breath in this world.

Sacred and irreplaceable days.

As I was saying, there was a plan that would never fail—because it would never begin: going together to the Gold Coast for my birthday. Amusingly, this plan began when our relationship was already ending—a plan born in the eye of the hurricane, where everything seemed calm.

Mysteriously, weeks after one May night, when my ex-enemy, through an Instagram message, declared that she would become my ex-ex-enemy, my two hands held the phone, its light casting cascading shades of blue over my face in the darkness—an inert lake under selenic rays. My eyes, like Thomas, needed to see the proof of what I already knew would happen but refused to believe. Blessed are those who have not seen and yet have believed.

Paraphrasing her own words, my beloved confirmed that it was best for us to separate once again. I, the unbeliever, touched my wounds, and they were real. Trembling fingerprints replied that I understood and accepted. A moment of emotion. The farewell. Her face, in my mind, became brighter and more beautiful than ever. Resignation translated into a click on the upper right corner of my iPhone. Darkness reigned. Eyelids closed. My head smothered the pillow. There were no tears.

I woke up the next day. The king had not yet risen, and a faint night still lingered in my room. 5:27 a.m. My face leaned towards the technological portal, the glow washing over me. I reread the conversation. My Lord and my God, what pain. Without further hesitation, I deleted the app that tied me to reality. I accepted. I moved on.

Her face still shone in my mind. Even now, as I write, it continues to shine.

Days passed. My energetic steps on the winter streets concealed my sadness—concealing something that no one cared about. No one knew me. As alone as never before, as alone as always. Solitude on my back, weighing down my shoulders, cautiously pulling my head backward—my chin held high—for now, it was my companion once again. Pride in my faithful companion.

And so, the days went by. I did not seek my ex-ex-enemy out of respect for her decision. Not that I lacked the desire, but—well, no need to explain. I was still in the rain bands; the worst was yet to come.

Returning to the weeks after this had happened, on a random night painted with ordinariness, I was making my way from the gym to my home. My thoughts, stupidly, revolved around the idea that my age had been the problem—the reason she had chosen to walk away again. I fought against this with the notion—still absolutely true even at this moment!

And one I would defend even before a judge—that despite my 34 years, I had more life and energy than any younger person, even those with better habits. Why? Simply because Pijao blood runs through my veins. Mentally, I do not know the meaning of the word fatigue. I am a machine built to survive capitalism, and to top it off, I am fucking irrational.

What stupid yet painfully real assertions. In the end, I was, I am, and I will always be a man of contradictions.

As the mountain ranges of my mind became drenched in these mists, without warning, two metres ahead, I noticed someone watching me. My neck turned slowly to the right, my pupils dilated, a billion hooves trampling through my veins. Her. Diagonal to me, her smile.

She walked straight ahead, and as if rehearsed, we both turned our torsos.

I greeted her.

"Her voice made perfume." She greeted me.

"Her breath made music." She said something.

I said something.

We each took a step forward.

Forty-seven seconds of interaction.

My hand on her waist, our eyes closed, her tongue in my mouth.

"Of all my senses joined in one."

Incomprehensible.

That night, she slept in my room.

A miracle.

O mystic metamorphosis!

Our chemistry was intact—Inconel and titanium—I don't know if that even exists, but it doesn't matter. We had no labels. My silent promise: *to do with her what spring does with the cherry trees!*

Even my lover, Solitude, sighed tenderly in its disbelief. Reason had no reason.

Relentlessly, without thinking, I was already proposing that we travel somewhere together for my birthday. She accepted with conviction.

Her essence—tungsten carbide—unconventional, extremely hard, but brittle.

Brittle under my unconscious pressure.

Oh, Solitude, treacherous lover, why didn't you stop me? Why did you let me be free!

For 168 hours and some minutes, constant winds fueled our interactions—unexpected calls, stupid little smiles after reading a notification on the phone, that "Good morning, how are you, amor", that "Sleep well, mamasita", going out for drinks—a warm fire introducing only comfort into the cold winter. The hope that this was a new beginning.

She, asleep in my bed beside me, the first hours of light breaking in, the lack of dark curtains allowing them to invade her privacy. Her soft breathing. Me, feeling that just by looking at her, I might disturb her dreams.

At that moment, my thoughts were on the young man who killed himself for Gretta—for what she had been before the marks of time, for the intensity of the moment.

My beloved kept sleeping, and I, now in the present, stare at the white ceiling of my room and think of Gabriel, Gretta's husband, who watched her grow old by his side and faced an absurd irony: someone destroyed himself for this woman, for the version of her that no longer exists, and he is there, in the words written by Joyce, watching her withered, worn by the years, feeling the weight of history, the inevitability of time.

I imagine him saying, "Fuck, how absurd all of this is." With an Irish accent, obviously.

That unspoken line, but one I assume he must have felt after that slap from fate: the love someone once destroyed themselves for was not eternal. What a painful revelation for that fictional Gabriel.

And now, I, in the past, watching my beloved sleep, wishing to see her like this no matter the years.

Love, after all—infinite, mysterious, and inexhaustible love.

We went dancing, and an older woman tried to dance with me, my beloved laughing and pushing me towards her, while in my own darkness, I wondered how many men in the past—like the one from the Dead—would have given everything for just one chance with her—and now, years before our eyes, had turned her into something comical.

We are fucking ignorant.

Ella y yo, qué ignorantes.

Anyway. Fun is fun.

My ex-enemy opened her eyes.

I told her, "Let's go for a coffee."

The last coffee we'd ever had together.

Fun is fun.

That Saturday, she wore my jeans and a red sweater. We looked incredible—hellishly sexy. It didn't matter what covered our skin; we stood out anywhere. The recurring topic of conversation was being someone special in each other's lives without labels. Going to the Gold Coast for my birthday, as I had already mentioned above, seemed like something Real, something Symbolic that would remain in the Imaginary. What a terrible joke. It was locked in, and without further hesitation, the hotels and flights were booked one or two days after she said goodbye to me that morning.

My life went on as it continues to this day and as it had before I met her—going to the gym, work, reading, writing, and filling with desires that void that lies in tomorrow, the impossibility of possibility. And of course, communicating with her was part of the equation of those days.

The following Wednesday night, after that Saturday, she called me at 8 p.m.

"Let's meet up, I'm leaving the gym."

"Alright, I'm leaving the gym too."

We met under the dim sky. The streets didn't look any different.

I wish I'd seen a black cat.

A shattered mirror.

Spilled salt. A ladder.

A rooster screaming into the shadows.

A fucking black butterfly—anything to warn me.

Anything to tell me: hold her tighter. Just a bit longer.

But everything seemed normal. We walked and laughed. Nothing felt out of place. It was fifty minutes or less. July. She said goodbye, and I said goodbye.

Why hold onto that moment? I would see her again.

The problem was that this was the last night I ever saw her.

Like magic, the intensity of our communication began to fade. I did my best, but I felt that she was already touching the wall of the hurricane's eye—she seemed so distant, as if she were floating in the cloud canopy.

I didn't know she could fly—and without warning, she escaped, untouched by the storm surge.

And I, who barely knew how to walk, not seeing her around me, tried calling her name—just to see if my voice could still reach her, if the wind could carry it to her ears.

Not even the echo replied.

I moved forward, following my instincts, and without realising it, I walked straight into the hurricane's eye wall.

Everything was overwhelmingly dense—I felt my body begin to levitate, and without warning, I was swept away.

Days of uncertainty followed.

I didn't know where I was or where I was going to end up, but one thing was clear:

She was already gone.

And I was still lost in the storm.

If the Hungarians went from producing scientists capable of destroying the world to becoming one of the greatest bastions of porn actresses in just a few decades, why should I feel completely delusional for one day believing that my ex-enemy and I would walk together through imminent mornings, letting the cold kiss our faces while bitter and precious coffee warmed our conversations? Why should that thought be any more absurd than waking up, scooping a spoonful of pre-workout, swallowing it dry—no water—only to receive that same morning cold, but in my soul?

On a crisp August morning, one that foretold the coming spring, after my delicious spoonful of pre-workout—dry, no water—and four missed calls to my ex-ex-enemy, along with a message the night before asking, "Are you seeing someone else?" I received her reply:

"Yes, I have been seeing someone; I don't want to lie to you. You knew this was going to happen—you had to know."

Mentally, I responded: "Yes, I knew."

On my phone screen, the words appeared:

"You are free. I just wanted to know..." that was my answer.

Why go into details? She told me she was confused, that she wanted me in her life but needed time and space.

What strange days followed. I tried to reach out, but I was a being without physical presence in her world—a ghost. But there was still the Gold Coast trip—that gave me some assurance that I would see her again soon.

A few weeks passed.

On Friday, 30 August, at 7:46 p.m. my phone vibrated.

I was reading. Solitude gripped my wrist firmly. I turned slowly, and we locked eyes. Its steady gaze rested beyond the emptiness of mine, a prophetess. Without speaking a word, in the language only it possesses, it told me:

"No social contact, no romantic ties. Nothing but your reading and me will be your company."

I swallowed hard and turned my damp eyes back to the book.

At 9:34 PM, Solitude kissed my neck, signaling that I was now free to check my phone.

The message was from her, of course.

"Amor, I am so sorry. I can't go to the Gold Coast with you."

"I think we should stop seeing each other."

Two messages.

I stood up.

Walked to the bathroom.

A drizzle began.

I returned to my room, remembering what Solitude had told me:

"No social contact, no romantic ties. Nothing but your reading and me will be your company."

Something was missing.

I didn't dwell on it.

I sat in front of my computer and, possessed by emotion, I wrote:

Friday, 30 August

In my mind is embedded the purple night when my body was swimming through the darkness of my room, weightless yet heavy. I sank into the chair and turned on my computer, but the dim light from the screen was swallowed by the shadows. Reaching for the lamp to my right—my steadfast companion of two years—I flicked it on. Its glow spilled across my fingers, revealing the worn letters on the keys. Outside, the drizzle tapped against the window, echoing the soft rhythm of my fingers on the keyboard. I felt as though the rain remembered the tears that once blurred my nights in solitude.

"No social contact, no romantic ties. Nothing but your reading, writing, and me will be your company."

That was her full sentence.

Today, September 10, one day before my birthday, I have obeyed with unwavering faith—the one who was with me before I entered this world, and the one who will leave with me when my time comes to depart.

I remember telling my ex-ex-ex-enemiga, on our very first date, that one of my greatest fears was leaving this world without having written a book.

But life is strange—mysterious in its unfolding.

Our minds capture the fleeting and the permanent, anchoring what once captivated or terrified us. A moment, a glance, a presence—something plants itself in the subconscious, takes root, and grows. It rises, quietly, until one day it ruptures the surface of our thoughts and becomes real—etched into the world, given form by our hands.

What wasn't there before now exists—brought to life through every keystroke, every press of a trembling finger.

Like now.

Creation demands inspiration. A shadow in the dark, once radiant.

And yes, I will always owe something to my ex-ex-ex-enemiga. Her mark on me, what she awakened—makes that old fear feel impossibly distant.

Thanks mamásita.

5:15 a.m. — My Birthday.

Happy fucking birthday to me.

Some had already gotten ahead of the game—corporate emails from places I didn't even know I was subscribed to, wishing me well, some with a coupon attached. What a magnificent start to this glorious day.

Since I moved to this part of the world, I've come to expect a few greetings: old acquaintances, the obligatory messages from uncles and aunts who used to demand responsibility and now just wish me health and prosperity. My closest friends message me too—their jokes, once mocking my screwups, now tinged with growing melancholy, though still funny. Then there's my mom, the video call, singing me "Feliz cumpleaños". Her face, more distant each year from the one my hands once touched— that is the day's peak.

My dad? He always texts two or three days later. And it's fine. More than welcome.

But here's the confession: like last year, and the year before that, I know—absolutely no one will give me a hug today. No one will say "Happy birthday" to me face-to-face.

That's the weight of solitude.

No one at work knows what day it is, and I won't lift a finger to bring it up. I barely have friends here, and to be honest, I don't want them. Contradictions. My own damn fault.

It's pathetic—no kiss on the cheek, no handshake, nothing. You'd have to be brain-dead to romanticise solitude. "I like being alone"—fuck off, idiots. You came into this world with the divine chance of sharing warmth, even if just for a few meaningless seconds. If you're lucky, you'll find someone who'll stay by your side—even if they annoy the hell out of you—until your last breath. If not, you'll sit on a park bench, smiling to the world but crying on the inside, aching to share a moment with someone. Then, after that, eternal drifting through the frozen, indifferent void of the universe.

You need balls—or ovaries—made of steel to survive that. And until you've felt it, really felt it, you have no idea what you're made of.

Even God felt disgust and pity for that ape Adam. So He gave him Eve—for the blessed pleasure of becoming someone. Because fuck—we need the other to complete the image of who we are.

Anerkennung. My fingers stumble typing it.

I am not fully myself without another who recognises me—or someone who recognises me for what I've done.

"Hey, look, it's the lonely writer." Shit, what a torture. It's almost laughable.

If we're surrounded by people who don't know who we are—just as unrecognisable to them as to ourselves—then in solitude, maybe we're nothing.

Or maybe we're everything.

Whatever the case, you better be built to withstand it.

But hey, maybe today's a wonderful day.

Maybe life will surprise me.

11:15 pm

Life did not surprise me.

Saying I was sick to skip work.

Going to watch the sunrise.

My mother's call.

Walking a lot, taking photos.

A message from my ex-ex-enemy: "happy birthday."

Replying to a few messages.

Coming back home, reading, doing this thing I'm doing now.

In a few hours, sleep.

Something of utmost importance—something that reveals either my confidence or my ignorance in the workings of fate—is the fact that I never cancelled the flights to the Gold Coast. Somewhere in my mind, I still believed life might surprise me.

The trip is set for 13 September. With only hours to go, and the odds are against me.

But I haven't lost faith.

Faith in what?

In everything.

Or in nothing."

VIII

"16 September 9:55 p.m.

Acá va una pequeña historia:

Three days ago, the sun—indifferent, half-veiled by clouds—watched me as I closed the door of my house, a bag slung over my shoulder. With unusual force, it pushed aside the stratus clouds, perhaps stirred by the faint trace of hope still lingering in my walk. Hope that her decision wasn't final. Hope for a tiny miracle. That somehow, she would appear—light breaking at the corner interrupted by her figure, her breath wrapping around my body, unintelligible words softly declaring she would join me.

I walked with that fantasy glowing in my head.

But at the bus stop, there was no silhouette. No dark hair. No intention.

Still, I boarded the bus with fragile optimism. I pictured her stepping in confidently at one of the stops before the airport. My mind saw her. My eyes did not.

Eventually, I drifted into sleep. And in the haze, a little devil whispered to me:

"She'll be at the airport. She knows the flight time. She'll surprise you."

I got off the bus. Each of my steps betrayed a truth I didn't want to accept—I was leaving her behind.

Yet I waited.

An hour passed.

I imagined the sterile air of the waiting lounge. I imagined her walking in, scanning the crowd, our eyes meeting, a story told in silence, and then the softest kiss.

Hope, distilled and sweet. Undiluted.

Already seated on the plane, a flight attendant approached.

Mid-sentence, she said her name.

And just like that, my secret came to light:

"She's not coming."

Silence followed.

No doubt her name had echoed through the halls of the airport.

But her ears never caught the sound.

The calls—once shouted by my voiceless soul—ceased the moment the plane left the ground.

It was awful not having her beside me. To see the empty space where she should've been.

I turned to the window. The edge of the world was painted orange and violet.

Blue, melting into a constellation of clouds.

There were no tears.

And for a moment—as infinite as the horizon blinking softly back at me—my heart heard the answer:

Close your eyes.

Try to sleep, little fool.

And I did.

I opened them just before landing.

And by then, it was already nostalgia.

Longing for something that never happened.

The temperature was around 22 degrees, maybe a little more. My first stop after leaving the airport was the bathroom, where I swapped my black sweater for a white shirt I had bought a few days earlier. I looked in the mirror and felt my spirits lift—a small ritual, but it worked.

Not wanting to complicate my night, I ordered an Uber to the hotel. It was a strange moment—the driver was talkative, surprisingly open. A man in his late forties, maybe early fifties, freshly divorced. His voice was lively, almost cheerful, as he told me his ex-wife was using their daughter to manipulate him. I thought about telling him my own situation—but instead, I offered a series of perfectly timed reactions: empathetic grunts, exaggerated surprise. In the rearview mirror, I was nothing but a well-behaved face, acting the part of a good listener. He seemed like a good man. I wanted to seem like one too.

I arrived at the hotel. Checking in alone was a quiet kind of torture, but the receptionist was empathetic—thankfully, no raised eyebrows, no comment about the missing companion. Twelfth floor. Balcony facing another building. A double bed with two towels folded at its edge. A bathroom with a bathtub. A coupon for two free drinks at the bar.

It was 9 p.m. I showered quickly, brushed my teeth, pulled on dark jeans, black boots, and tucked the white shirt into my pants like a gentleman. A black belt. One spray of cologne. A swashbuckling pirate, ready for high-seas adventure.

My guardian angel stood to my left. Solitude, filing its nails on the bed, looked up and said, "Go out and enjoy yourself, sexy motherfucker. Tonight, you're free."

I smiled, felt flattered. But as soon as the elevator doors opened and the three mirrors greeted me, I realised it again—I was devilishly sexy. The kind of allure that doesn't care about symmetry. My walk, my face, my body, my nostalgia, my poverty, my dreams, who I was and who

I will be—everything about me was seduction wrapped in melancholy. An inexhaustible source of fleeting romanticism. I could already picture a hot blonde telling her friend, *don't let me go with that bald ugly guy... but he's so sexy.*

I hadn't even claimed my two free drinks, and my own perception was already aligning with reality—because, yes, I am fucking sexy. It didn't matter that I was sinking into emotional mud. Even that is sexy on me. And don't get me started on my arrogance—pure, unapologetic eroticism.

Four lychee martinis in 17 minutes. No food since the day before. 9:10 p.m.

Phone at 76%.

Passport in pocket.

Ego at 150%.

What could possibly go wrong?

What a beautiful night embraced me. The stars, drowned out by the excess of man-made light—thousands of artificial glows, each hiding its own silent narrative.

Inside, the alcohol tricked me into emotional clarity—an illusion, yes, but I had surrendered my critical judgment hours ago. With no food in my stomach, the biochemical mirage made me feel strangely aligned with myself—my thoughts, my memories, my illusions. I was ready to make impulsive, emotionally charged decisions, believing each one carried some sacred mission.

A storm of false lucidity, born of erratic introspection.

My plan for the night?

To end it by devouring an entire pizza, blackout drunk, on some park bench—savouring it even more, as drunkenness often turns the absurd into the divine. All around me, specters of the night would be babbling about their own little triumphs and calamities—this shared odyssey of beautiful bastards. And I'd wake the next morning with no clue how it all ended—just the aftertaste of pepperoni and mystery.

I walked into the first convenience store I saw and bought a bottle of water, a Red Bull, and a pack of gum. Admirably, I paid for everything—completely sober, I probably would've stolen it all with zero shame. What kind of drunk was I? What a disgrace.

Without overthinking it, I scanned the street for a place to enter. The water was gone in three gulps; the Red Bull timidly remained in my back pocket. It was exhausting to see so many people lining up outside clubs, rows and rows of them, each one trying to be more glamorous than the next—like the prized cattle awaiting auction. But it was necessary. I had to be one of them, blend into the herd.

I passed by the flashiest venues, each guarded by the most ridiculously dressed bouncers I had ever seen—

skinny pants, leather shoes with no socks, shirts about to explode from the pressure of their gym-toned chests.

Deus meus, Deus meus, ut quid dereliquisti me?

But then, miraculously, Fate—always high on irony— had something in store for me. After walking the whole street, back and forth, unable to decide where to insert my presence, I randomly—swear to God—stopped about two metres from the entrance of one of the most packed clubs on the strip. A group of about ten men, uniformed like cult members of some secret ritual, jumped the long line. Their leader whispered confidently to the runway-Italian-model-type pretending to be a bouncer.

One by one, my new best friends walked in—no IDs checked. And I, the virgin, walked into the clearing, uninvited, and found myself at the centre of a coven's aquelarre.

My white shirt, the brainlessness of my new companions, and perhaps a coin tossed somewhere by fate had worked in my favour. Heads or tails—it didn't matter. Fifteen minutes later, I was in the VIP section of the bar, drunkenly shouting the lyrics to a 50 Cent song I didn't even know.

They even gave me a wristband so I could enter and exit the VIP section without hassle. It felt absurdly official for someone barely clinging to coherence. I went to the bar, ordered two drinks, and handed one off at random—like it was holy water shared from a chalice of sin. It was as if the excess saliva on the glass gave it mystical properties. Nothing mattered anymore. What a disgrace. Or maybe just the ritual of the damned.

I felt like I was standing at the edge of an abyss. My mind was veiled in ethanol mist. Red lights melted through the air, and my mouth had stopped producing saliva—vodka was doing the job instead. I could already feel the night starting to collapse.

Then, out of nowhere, someone dropped their arm over me, anchoring me in a sloppy rite of brotherhood. The one I assumed was their leader hugged me and said something I couldn't decipher. He was speaking in slurred tongues; I responded by poorly singing whatever song was playing. He held me tighter, and with another guy by his side, gestured for me to follow. They summoned me like a stray dog they'd just adopted.

We slid across the dance floor like men on a mission, headed towards the bathroom. A bell didn't ring—but the word "bathroom" was enough. I started to salivate like Pavlov's mutt.

Our reflections greeted us like guiltless clones, blurry and amused. The three of us crammed into a stall. A gleaming bag, full of war and the rot of my country, sparkled.

Benzoylmethylecgonine cut with Panadol.

!Perico hijueputa!

The last time I'd done it was with my ex-ex-enemy, during a white night of the past. What a blessed night that had been.

The bag was full. I was offered the first line. I snorted. The chemical slid down my throat—sharp and bitter, like betrayal. I tasted the shame of misrepresenting my country. They were using a mini spoon.

A surge of personal power. I whipped out my house key like a knight unsheathing his blade and showed them how it's easier—and hotter—using it. They laughed like they'd known me for years. Beautiful idiots. Brothers.

Four times I dipped the key. Four nostrils were cursed. We high-fived. I was one of them. I had been baptised.

They trusted me—their fellow initiate. They left me the sacred bag. The euphoria was so intense that for a second, I believed it too. I believed they were my real friends.

I checked their noses for powder and led us out. The pact was inked in white.

¡Qué buen amigo!

Six minutes later, I was on the street.

Alone.

The whole bag in my possession.

My greatest act of fraternity? Saving them from more cocaine. Teaching them a lesson. A true act of love, really. You're welcome, hermanos.

Giving them a story to talk about in the future.

The party had just begun.

The mere idea of my ex-comrades going out to look for me added exuberance to my predicament—it almost amused me, to be honest. I didn't really give a fucking shit. Without much urgency, I looked for another place. The absence of liquor in my mouth began to bother me, and the urge to snort again had gone from temptation to necessity.

Despite the street being packed with people, I found a shadowy corner where I shamelessly did two discreet bumps, courtesy of my already-mentioned blade. Clarity entered me—the damn filthy chemical—its postnasal drip dragging the compound right where taste and guilt are most perceptible.

There were still many options to continue the night, but none felt appealing. I walked a bit more until I stepped into a convenience store where I bought a bottle of water and, for no reason at all, a blue vape: blueberry pomegranate. Three puffs while walking—and I felt ridiculous.

My mind was outrunning my steps, and before I realised it, I was standing in front of an Irish pub. The kind of place where the leftovers from other clubs ended up, dragged in by the night's inertia. No line. The bouncer barely glanced at me and waved me through.

A live band was playing late '90s classics, pop-punk and 2000s indie rock, giving it their all on stage. I must admit, the vibe inside was way better than the last club. I was desperate for a drink, but my bladder was begging to be emptied, and my nose was pleading to be filled.

I came out of the bathroom lighter in fluids, heavier in lucidity. My jaw was doing that thing again—some grotesque samba only substances know how to choreograph. I needed a drink quickly to blend in among the drunks.

I bought a beer and a shot of tequila—I thought I was invincible.

Idiot.

Certified.

A few steps, dodging people, beer at waist level, and I was already humming Somebody Told Me by The Killers. It was impressive—everyone in the bar was singing it like their lives depended on it.

But I wasn't ok.

Paranoia crept in.

Back to the bathroom.

As soon as I walked in, two tall men were talking. I was more shamelessness than person. In front of them, I pulled out the bag. They looked at me. I looked at them. My lip curled into a smirk, my right hand holding the key, offering a seductive motion.

They exchanged a glance.

Silence.

All three of us locked eyes.

Subtitles at the bottom of the screen: "Why not."

The sway of the door let in a pop song about friends getting higher than the Emp—

The Tower of Babel!

Coincidence? Fuck, no!

Cut to: the three of us stumbling out of the bathroom, arms around each other.

"You are the man!"

"Yes, you are!"

The celebration roared back to life.

I had given them only the tip of the key—a bit of love. I felt so good doing that, I repeated the act several times with different people. I seemed like I could multiply fish and bread in micrograms—tiny doses that won me disciples. From nobody to a legend in under an hour.

Hell, I even blessed a bouncer.

Until my brain went into revolution and told me:

"You idiot. Save some for us."

And just like that, generosity gave way to greed.

The night was merging deeper into my plasma, messing with me, cell by cell. I was getting sick of the place—of the people around me, of the music. I needed air. But first, I snorted a bit of clarity and took a drink—some leftover concoction handed to me by one of my many friends.

Suddenly, I was in the smoke area. I leaned against the railing overlooking the street, placed the vape in my mouth, inhaled the vapour without letting it pass my throat, and exhaled slowly, releasing thick aromatic clouds into my aura.

I imagined a world without gravity.

She and I in another galaxy, floating in ecstasy, treating each other like a fantasy.

I stayed there like that for a few minutes— *ella y yo,* orbiting in lust, mirroring each other's desires.

Thinking about the fairest of the fair.

A faceless woman approached and asked if she could use my vape. Without looking at her, I handed it over. She took three drags before handing it back. She asked me something. My answer, still not looking at her: "Escaping the mind is impossible." She repeated my phrase, let it sit in her mouth like I had with the smoke.

"You are so much fun," she said after a beat of silence.

It was time to go. I went to the bar and asked for a beer before leaving. The bartender, a young woman with beautiful tired eyes and chipped black nail polish, stared at me intensely as she poured the bubbling potion. And in my dilated gaze, she saw the pupils of my beloved—looking at me after doing a line of cocaine on my bedroom desk some months ago.

"Why the nostalgia?" she asked.

Nostalgia and melancholy—fucking words, like Cain's mark, following me till the end.

My answer: "Escaping the mind is impossible."

She didn't flinch. Smiled.

Instead, she poured two shots of Jameson.

Pushed one towards me.

Raised hers.

I raised mine.

We toasted.

And instantly—I felt it.

A knot in my gut.

A wave of nausea crashing over the moment.

My eyes watered, betraying a different story than the one I meant to live.

I left the beer untouched on the bar.

Bolted out the door.

Found refuge in a narrow, unlit alleyway.

And there it arrived.

A torrent of lifeless liquid shot from my mouth—water, stomach acid, alcohol in a dozen shades. My gift to the earth. A bitter part of me spilled on concrete.

I looked up at the sky in search of stars—there wasn't a single one.

No appetite. No sleep. No idea what I was feeling, but something told me I had to go back to the hotel.

Anyone watching me walk that night, so upright, so nonchalant, would never have suspected the infernal party raging in my head.

Once inside, I remembered I had broken the promise I made to myself: to eat pizza under the moon.

It didn't matter anymore.

Already in the room, I blasted music from my phone, convinced it would wake the entire hotel.

What a fool—music didn't even wake my soul, which by that hour had already gone to sleep.

It was just me, flesh and bone.

A snap of fingers echoed in my mind when I remembered there was a bathtub.

Without hesitation, I started to fill it. My last hit of the night would be taken submerged. The idea was so satisfying, it needed something more.

Inside my suitcase was Tomorrow in the Battle Think on Me by Javier Marías.

What a title. What a curse.

Last year, a random Google search told me Marías had died on September 11, 2022. I took it as a divine sign, and without hesitation, bought A Heart So White. What a fucking masterpiece—not the best book I've read, but certainly my favourite.

Sensual, dreamlike, elegant.

I grabbed the book and, for reasons I still haven't deciphered, stepped into the tub fully clothed.

The fabric clung to my skin.

Every soaked fibre revealed every fold, every line, every curve.

The weight of my jeans multiplied; the water trapped between layers became a slow-moving armor.

The colour of the denim deepened, exposing a more intimate version of itself.

My white shirt turned sheer.

What was hidden was now suggested.

Naturally, I had left the bag of snow and the vape outside—melancholic sensuality and symbolism had nothing on my instinct for preserving vice.

One hit—right nostril—just enough to burn.

Let it rip the flesh if needed, let the water stain red.

The vape was next, its flavored smoke crawling into my lungs like a velvet curse. My head fell back. I raised the book with trembling hands, careful not to soak it in the filth I'd chosen. Half a sentence—no more. I wedged the little bag between the pages like a sacrament, a mark of some forgotten ritual. Then pushed the book away, just out of reach, like all things I once tried to hold but couldn't.

Outside the bathroom, my phone was playing some version of "The Unforgiven" by Metallica.

My eyes closed.

Exhaustion consumed me. I didn't fall asleep. I simply remained in a state of stillness for a few minutes. I got out of the bathtub, peeled off my clothes slowly, left them in a corner, stepped out of the bathroom, dried myself at an unhurried pace, turned off the lights, and, under the sheets—hid my nakedness.

My loyal phone, with only 2% battery left, did the impossible to wake me up at 8 a.m. Its alarm rang beyond the valley of shadows where I lay, pulling me out of my dreamless sleep. I was annoyed at first, but later thankful— I was still in time for the hotel buffet, and I was starving.

I got up, threw on some blue jeans, a black shirt, and my boots—which, fortunately, I hadn't submerged the night before.

What a goddamn feast I had. No less than five scrambled eggs, hash browns spilling off my plate, fruit and absolutely everything that should never be on the same plate—drenched in BBQ sauce. The orange juice added a touch of moderation to the mountain of food I set before me.

Amazingly, I had no hangover and was full of energy. I knew I still had some nose candy left in the bag—and allegedly plenty of dignity.

Back in the room, I resisted the Diablo's temptation. It was 10:47 a.m., and the hotel bar wouldn't open until noon, but my inner Bukowski was already gallivanting off through barley-flavoured delusions, beneath the mischievous, beautiful sun pouring through the terrace.

The perfect excuse to keep him chained: my phone needed to be fully charged before setting sail.

I didn't want to waste time, so I started doing push-ups and various exercises as if preparing for a personal vendetta. I showered, groomed myself—I was dressed to the nines, dressed to kill. Same clothes I wore to breakfast, yet I looked fantastic. Slight dark circles under my tanned face gave me that nocturnal charm that drives people crazy, mate!

11:46 a.m.—I was walking out of the hotel. The surroundings weren't lively: families with noisy kids everywhere, a few pubs with no spark. I went to the beach. Got bored. Got bored. Got bored—until I fled.

Wandering beneath the buildings, I saw a group of people lining up at an elevator. My curiosity lined up with them. I entered in the third round. I was right—it was an exclusive rooftop entertainment complex. It looked quite good. There was music and alcohol. I paid $25 to get in, got a hideous orange wristband, and after seventeen steps I was at the bar.

A blonde beer—for the sake of moderation. I didn't want to look like a lost foreigner, so I minimised my movements before settling into a spot facing one of the pools. Women in swimsuits sunbathing, tattooed muscular men—a copy of a copy. But the vibe was actually good, it had a luxurious touch, and I was the stain that gave it spice.

I swear I wasn't drunk—I had only one beer—when a meteorite of an idea crashed mercilessly into my sanity, annihilating all current thoughts:

"Victor, sign up for the skydiving course."

My mind spun wildly around that idea until it became a desire. A real desire. Tangible. Another beer to sharpen the view. I already had a rough idea of the cost—I'd played with the thought before. I used the calculator, checked my bank accounts—it became more and more feasible. I could already see myself flying. I could see myself requesting vacation days. I checked possible options: WA, Queensland, NSW. Prices. How to get there. Numbers.

Why not?

Why yes?

Another beer.

More poured in.

A hot blonde smiling at me—maybe at the handsome guy behind me—didn't matter. I could see myself jumping from the plane alone. I felt fear. Adrenaline. What if something goes wrong? But it's really safe.

I pictured myself with the licence. I saw myself in third person, Kickstart My Heart by Mötley Crüe blasting in the background. It felt so real. It had to be.

Why not?

A town called M-, six hours from Sydney by bus. The course lasted 7 days, 15 jumps. I filled out the online form.

Name.

Age.

Why?

I didn't even know.

"I did it once and fell in love with the experience," I quickly typed.

What if I die?

Obviously won't happen, right?

Available start dates: Monday, 21 October—exactly a month away.

"¡Sí, qué hijueputas!"

Send.

Smiling screen:

"Thank you. We'll review your application and get in touch."

I was sweating. It was intense.

Another beer.

A trip to the bathroom.

A phone notification—an email. I opened it nervously.

Congratulations Victor,

We are stoked to confirm your acceptance into our Accelerated Free-Fall (AFF) course!

Nothing available for 21 October, but the link below will show all available dates.

To secure your spot, follow the link and pay the $1,100 deposit.

[link]

My God.

What do I do?

My God…

"Si se metio de puta a culear."

What a crude way of saying I couldn't back out anymore.

Another beer.

No more beer until I decided.

It's now or never.

"Yo no nací el día de los temblores."

I opened the link. October 14—wasn't going to wait any longer.

I filled in the card details.

Pay.

Click.

Breathe slowly.

The world had stopped spinning.

One email made it spin again:

Hi Victor,

Thanks for booking with Sky… Your order R5DPNDW is confirmed.

If you have any further questions about your order, please contact the Customer Service Team at 130…

I smiled—afraid.

And went to get a cold vodka soda.

Two shots, please.

The reckless yet predictable—for those who know me—decision to sign up for the course slowly dissolved under the sunlight and the small sips of various drinks I was enjoying. What had once seemed like a difficult and complex choice was now overshadowed by a far simpler one: calamari and chips or pulled pork nachos. The squid killed the pig.

The food wasn't extraordinary, but the aioli bumped it up to 8 out of 10 stars. It also helped dilute the delicious grip alcohol had on my bloodstream.

Suffocated by the relaxed atmosphere, I decided to head back to the hotel—there, I could let the sun rest from my presence and conceal my now very noticeable loneliness.

It was still early—3:44 p.m. I remember evaluating the situation while sitting on the terrace of the room, drinking coconut water. Coconut water I had bought before entering the hotel—nothing appears magically in this story. Despite everything that had happened, I was still thinking of her.

The scenes in my mind with her in this place were worthy of future study by a new race of humans—beings whose rationality had reached the point of being unable to see the sublimity of love—or the raw ache of carnal desire. They would want to understand the phenomenon for which they'd already have a boring, logical explanation, but which they'd be unable to feel.

Quick notes. Speculative glances. Clinical questions for the expert on duty. Physiological reactions triggered in them as they watched us dance across different worlds— bluish and red lights igniting the room, her and me half-naked on the hotel bed, drunk, singing what they'd call "old music," while kisses and whisky covered our bodies.

Tension building with a tug of the hand, a bold approach, a masterfully lewd whisper in the ear followed by a gentle bite to the lobe. A subtle push—one of us collapsing backward while the other watches in delirium. The prey defenseless, the predator hiding the urgency, like an avalanche promising to unleash unspoken intimacy—

only to graze the body, confess half-breathed erotic darkness, and retreat slowly without breaking eye contact.

Glistening trails of sweat branded her abdomen—my signature without permission.

The victim's skin felt fingernails tearing the air, grazing the flesh. The walls sweating. Laughter, sensuality, complicity. Her mouth licking my abdomen. Pink nipples begging to be kissed. Our positions shifting. A brush of lips that sets fire to everything! To nothing! To us!

The now not-so-innocent students of the future understanding, in their gut, what's happening. Me, licking the fibers of her underwear, inhaling the soft saltiness—like skin after desire under the sun. Blessed liquid. Warmth and wetness within me. Damp earth and the slow blooming of a savage flower in her.

My eyes closed, her swirling tongue triggering nervous contractions through my entire being. Her taste and mine blending into a passionate and infernal kiss. The lights go out. Class is over. The evolved beings look at each other— anguish and curiosity. Some lower their gaze.

Biology—or a miracle.

A few clouds drift above, which my libido-drenched mind compares to the ink of desire.

The afternoon sank reluctantly. Before the sunlight could escape, I went out again and bought an entire pizza with garlic bread—my offering to the dusk. I returned to the same dull beach. My fingers were soaked in greasy cheese as my eyes locked onto an unstable horizon, painted in desperate oranges and fading fire. I cursed myself for not buying something to drink—then laughed at the irrelevance of thirst when hunger ruled with such reckless power. Every bite was consumed like a swain devoured in the shadows, just as night swallowed the day without mercy. A nearby fountain quenched my thirst and rinsed the glistening sins from my hands.

Darkness had summoned the same creatures as the night before—different faces, same repeated fates. I walked into a bottle shop. The spiced rum chose me. Back in the room, I ritualistically cleansed my insides, my body, my soul. Half a glass of rum—almost threw up. A perfect line across the book. A quick inhale with a five-dollar bill. Head thrown back. Grains stuck somewhere inside—it did not matter. I welcomed it

And after another full glass of rum, I said goodbye to my room.

Farewell, sanity.

A scrumptious night and a delish Sunday that must not be narrated now—to preserve the mystique.

I returned Monday on a noon flight, once again with an empty seat beside me. My thirty-fifth spring had ended: good anecdotes, a skydiving course on the horizon, ambrosia, decadence, and sensory opulence left clinging to my skin.

With my routine welcoming me with open arms, and me kissing it in desperation, this little story ends.

Blessed routine—so rigid, so necessary.

"Nor love thy life, nor hate; but what thou liv'st

Live well, how long or short permit to Heav'n."

That's what the archangel Michael told Adam after the fall—stoic wisdom wrapped in Christian resignation. To live well is to have a purpose, to love, and to indulge in a few vices. I won't bore you with the details; I'll just say that in these past few days, I've been sharpening my routine— making it more productive. Skydiving videos playing while I hit my core workouts at the gym. Writing and writing. Reading and reading. And feeling a deep, abhorrent disgust towards social media.

I wonder if, in those visions of humanity's future that Mike showed the first ape, he included this: that to live fully in the year 2024 would mean being glued to a phone, watching people pretend to be happy, wishing to pretend to be happy so that someone else might wish for that same happiness—and so on, endlessly.

That his paternal and ancient voice, almost cracked with time, whispered the answer to what the modern human wants—or believes they want: to have everything, experience everything, live everything.

And with a smile that shimmered with tenderness—pity, really—the kind only an older brother who has witnessed pain can give, who has seen the beginning and knows the end, he revealed that there would be no need to bite into some tempting and forbidden fruit.

Merely seeing an image on a screen—an image of what the standard says must be desired, lived, experienced—would be enough.

And the first Homo sapiens sapiens, upon seeing those prophetic images of beings like himself holding luminous devices in their hands, simply turned to the winged man and asked where he could get one of those.

A dastardly loop, really. Beautifully packaged. Lovingly marketed. Spiritually bankrupt.

And still, despite the disgust, some part of me was already agog—hungry for something unexpected, some signal or whisper in the dark paradise.

I've been trying to stay away. Deleted the apps from my phone. Kept my distance.

Until today— X October.

The birthday of the fairest of the fair.

Spring Sunday.

She knows a message from me will reach her today. I know a message from me will reach her today. The person reading this knows a message from me will reach her today.

It's obvious.

My phone is downloading Instagram as I type this. The pink icon appears. I grab the phone with my right hand and keep typing with the left. I laugh at how stupid I sound narrating every action with such *pointillism*.

I use "I" too much; it's sad.

It amuses me, so I won't delete it.

I'd love to have the talent of the greats—those who, when describing the mundane, can suddenly evoke a physical or even metaphysical sensation.

But the weight of the phone doesn't change.

Its texture doesn't burn my fingers.

Its light doesn't soothe my soul.

There's no flash of the past giving this moment a thousand layers of meaning. I only feel a near-divine restlessness and curiosity about what I'll say—and whether she'll reply.

No blood came out of my nose.

I didn't face a thousand demons or my most hidden fears.

There was no dialogue between my id, ego, and superego—or maybe there was.

But from my fingers, this exploded:

Hey… happy birthday… I want to tell you something but now's not the time…

Send.

I'd like to tell her something more. I have a hunch. Maybe I want to say goodbye because something's about to happen?

It's not impossible. Everything will be fine.

But maybe I should say more—what if this is the last chance?

Last chance.

Nothing's going to happen.

You should say something more—something might happen.

No, nothing's going to happen.

She's busy.

Yes, but… why the fuck do I feel like I have to say goodbye if everything is fine?

And for five or ten minutes, my mind spun in that dialogue.

I had to act. But how? Like Odysseus, stupid!! What you mean?

You hear the siren song and instead of plugging your ears like a bitch, you tie yourself to the mast and yeet the app into digital oblivion.

I deleted the damn app, leaving the message just like that.

Anyway—why say goodbye if everything was going to be fine?

Roguery mind!

It really scares me not to say goodbye.

But nothing's going to happen!!

It's been six days since I sent the message. In an hour, I fly to Sydney. I'm at the airport, writing in public for the first time. There are only a few people around me, but every time someone passes by, I get the feeling their shadow glances at my screen, and because of that, I don't dare write that the idea of downloading Instagram again fills me with a strange mix of fear and guilt.

At first, I felt strangely comfortable inside that tension. But now, with just minutes to go before I head to Sydney — to spend the night with friends, probably drinking — and then catch a 9 a.m. bus tomorrow to M- from Central Station. I feel something else. The trip will be long: six or seven hours by bus, maybe followed by a walk, a taxi, or whatever it takes to reach the drop zone. I'll rest for a bit, and on Monday, I'll begin. First instructions, then one to three jumps depending on the weather, accompanied by instructors. I saw it all on YouTube.

And here's where I spoiled the excitement: from the very first jump, it will be just the instructors beside me during free fall. The landing, though, will be mine alone — guided from the ground by radio. Eventually, I'll jump with no one holding on, just an instructor in the sky watching to see if I've internalised what was taught on solid earth.

All of this… without contacting her. Without even checking if she replied to my message. Of course, there's a part of me that doesn't want to face whatever she might've said — or didn't say. But I'd love to tell her what I'm about to do.

Still, I have to accept that something in me — something buried deep — tells me this is mine. Entirely mine. That saying anything more would only stir up unnecessary drama. That she might see it as a pathetic attempt to draw her attention.

And yes… while I was writing this pseudo-philosophical self-restraint monologue, the app finished downloading.

Spoiler: she reacted to the message with a heart.

Anyway, time to board the plane."

I read this segment quite quickly, I think I skipped lines between yawns. I don't really feel sleepy—it's more of a bodily reflex triggered by the blurry hour now flickering on my screen. I close my eyes and, upon opening them, see my arm reaching for the glass of water. After a few sips, I start thinking about the personality dripping through this text—borderline, melancholic-existential, sublimated romantic dependence. It's soaked in it. I smirk at myself for labelling it that way. Over time, my view of it—and of its narrator—has changed. I feel like he lies a lot. His behaviour during the breakup, that obsessive aftermath, is irrational.

If she said, "It's over," and he just replied, "I understand and respect your decision," I don't believe him, and I never will.

I've got my own theory of what really happened—a theory that's changed over the years.

When I first read it, I can see myself saying, "Mate… I don't know if this guy's heartbroken or just off his head on metaphors. Like—is it deep, or is he just saying heaps of weird shit 'cause he's sad?"

That while drinking a Red Bull in front of my computer.

Pathetic. I hadn't understood half of what I'd read. All those references I completely missed.

References I only began to grasp later— like when I was thirty-six and read Ada or Ardor, and in the introduction, it said Nabokov had been an entomologist. That thirty-six-year-old me felt a strange admiration for this tragic-lucid lover.

Sixteen years just to smile at a sentence.

Worse yet, when I faced my first heartbreak years later, I realised I hadn't known the highs or the lows of emotion back then. I had mocked the author when I was 20, thought I was above him—and years later, I dragged myself through that same cognitive filth.

What a moment…

I need to stop remembering, return to now.

Every eternity I spend in memory is one more minute closer to sunrise, and I want to finish the text.

I definitely won't read it tomorrow—or maybe I will—but I want to end the night with the sense that I saw it through.

There's only one part left—the one that truly led me to search for Victor… and how I ended up meeting her. But before that, something interrupts his manuscript in the most unexpected way:

Right in the middle of the narrative, without warning or explanation, there appears a complete draft of a book—written entirely in Spanish. As far as I've been able to find, it was never published. The first time I read through the file, I skipped it— I didn't speak the language. But over time, I began translating it, line by line, word by word. Editing, questioning, decoding.

It doesn't seem to relate directly to Victor's story. And yet… it's there. I've been meaning to finish it. I will. It deserves to be seen.

Its title is:

Sangre

———

But not tonight.

Not now.

Right now, I need to return to the reason
I came here in the first place.

I'll skip over it again—just for now, as
I did the first time.

I want to reach the ending.

To see how it all comes together.

To finally—tonight, maybe before dawn—
finish the story.

IX

"I've just arrived in M- a few hours ago. It's Sunday, 13 October. What can I say? Last night I met up with a few friends. A few beers; or many, depending on one's perspective—enough to wake up this morning with a slight headache. My breakfast was at Macca's with my dear friend, who accompanied me all the way to Central Station to catch the bus that brought me here. With crumbs of bread around the corners of my lips and my mouth steaming with the toasted and bitter taste of the day's first heartbeat, there was a faint edge of saudade when we said goodbye—within the dark, earthy, and slightly acidic flavor of the coffee we'd had, unspoken memories of the past hung between us, and a warm promise lingered to see each other the following week when I returned with my skydiving licence.

The bus ride wasn't anything out of the ordinary—various stops, towns without much difference, ocean, houses, bush, people getting on and off, shots of my face in profile, absorbed in something beyond what the landscape offered. At four-something in the afternoon, I got off the bus and went straight to the local Woolies to stock up on "provisions." To my dismay, the place where the course would be held was a 7-minute drive away. Alright then — let's order an Uber! No Uber service! A taxi or a bus? No taxis or buses either! 90 minutes walking!

With my bag on my shoulder, I walked along the road until I reached the place where, at this very moment, in the room they had ready for me, I sit writing. My black boots, under the spring sun of NSW, gave me some beautiful blisters on the area of the Achilles tendon. The right one burst from the friction of the walk, leaving a sensual bloodstain on my nearly torn socks; the left one, throbbing with masochistic delight, begging for the pleasure of rupture, left a little stream of reddish water across my pale skin.

My consolation: a protein shake, a slow-cooked beef brisket ready in just 25 minutes, and before sleeping, a few lines written by the saint of my devotion, Clarice Lispector. I had no complaints — the site had clean bathrooms, a well-equipped kitchen, a place to fraternise with my future course mates, and a small, cozy room — enough to contain the fear of what tomorrow will bring.

It's worth noting that I've already fraternized with two people as soon as I arrived: a long-haired man from Queensland whose name I've already forgotten despite the fact he told me only half an hour ago, and a Canadian woman who works here whose name, thanks to my ever-reliable lack of attention, I also don't recall. In any case, I've

now painted a little portrait of my soul with the keyboard—
bon appétit and sweet dreams to me!

14 October greets me with a dawn so imposing that I'm almost irritated there are no roosters around to give it the tribute it deserves. 5:45 a.m. — the horizon looks like freshly roasted lamb, carved without delay, its scarlet juices spilling across the table rather than onto the impatient diner's taste buds. I woke up far too early. The first class begins at 8:30 a.m., but I did it on purpose. I've designed a routine for this week of training: read the current book, do a light workout, cook a healthy—though not abundant— breakfast, call my mother (the time difference is perfect), and write about how I'm experiencing this first day, which will probably feel redundant by tomorrow.

Fear has turned into anticipation. From what I understand, today will be an in-depth introduction into how everything works—what one faces when jumping out of a plane from 15,000 feet, the obvious and not-so-obvious malfunctions, and how not to perish on the first attempt... or the second... or the third.

My heart beats with desperation.

The day has come.

7:35 p.m., I survived my first day! Zero jumps, almost eight hours of ground instruction and training—these people take it very seriously, something wonderful but also something that raises the tension and, therefore, the fear and anticipation of what's coming tomorrow. Our instructor, Matt, a cool guy in his forties who has dedicated his life to skydiving—over 7,000 jumps. It's funny, but in this environment, the number of jumps replaces your last name. I really enjoyed today's class. My classmates, as I mentioned yesterday, include a young guy from Queensland with long hair, whose name I still don't remember—a good person outwardly, but a bit pretentious. Look who's talking. A woman from Victoria, whose name I also forgot. Glen, a man in his sixties with whom I chatted for a while, more Australian than Vegemite. According to his story, he skydived back in the 2000s but had to stop due to life circumstances, and to resume now, he had to take the course again. And lastly, another man whose name I also forgot, from Wollongong—his job: wedding singer. I remember everyone's last name, except Glen's. Zero jumps. I feel mentally exhausted. Tomorrow's going to be a big day!!

Tuesday, 15 October.

Rewind.

Play.

No sunrise this time—just a dull sky and the sound of repetition.

My last name tonight will be 1 jump—or maybe 4 jumps.

How thrilling.

It's 7:37 pm, I'm in my room, and my narrating what's about to come would be an apotheotic spoiler, because quite literally, I shouldn't be the one telling it.

At exactly 8:38 am we were already standing in front of Matt, with a giant smile across his face and in his right hand a cup of coffee, swinging rhythmically to the cadence of his animated speech. Without further ado, he introduced us to the other instructors: Bronte, with over 1500 jumps; Clark, her husband, 3000 jumps; and Bill, a stoic-looking man with 5000 jumps. Peter, the pilot and owner of the place, with over 17,000 jumps. The bastard had spent more time in the air than on solid ground. All of them inspired confidence. My body entered a state of unimaginable alertness. I felt like every move I made was driven by something beyond my rational mind. I was given a helmet with a built-in radio, through which I would receive instructions while in the air, an altimeter, and a suit tailored to my well-sculpted body. The moment was approaching. If you saw me from someone else's eyes, I probably looked calm, walking towards the prep area, a mix of focus and contained adrenaline in each step. Matt handed me the harness, and though my hands should've been trembling, they took it firmly, and I nonchalantly smiled, thanking him. I put it on like stepping into another skin—legs in, a pull upwards, arms sliding in, another burden on my back, another tension on my nervous system. The metal clips locked with force, pressure on my chest and my loins. Each click sounded like a war drum. I adjusted the straps with decisive movements, pulling hard to feel the gear fuse with my body. Bill checked that I was doing it right. The pilot was already in the plane, engines starting. The silence in my mind collapsed. Check, double-check. The sun, resting on a cloud, waiting for the show, its rays falling like lead over the runway. My mouth tasted of salt, I felt the sweat on the fabric, my armpits betraying the calm look on my face—luckily, no one could see. I'd be jumping with Matt and Clark on my first attempt, and Jack, the young guy from Queensland whose name I hadn't remembered, would jump with Bill and Bronte. We were the chosen ones for this dopamine feast.

Jack—a name I'll never forget.

As I'd said before, I'd already done two tandem jumps, one of them with my ex-enemiga. I must admit, I thought about her a lot during that first jump. The experience was fairly similar. The engine noise cutting through any sound brave enough to compete. Already crammed into the plane, as it took off, I kept staring at the altimeter—paranoia. I imagined telling Matt, "No mate, I changed my mind, I don't want to jump." I rehearsed it in my head. I saw myself saying it. The plane kept climbing. I swear I was going to say, "I can't, I changed my mind, I don't want to jump."

A full mental war.

Who knows how many neurons died in that war.

But when the engine noise was overtaken by the roar of the wind rushing in as the door opened—it was like an H-bomb over my thoughts. Before I knew it, I was at the door. Matt outside, Clark inside, me staring at the horizon. My voice against the wind: "horizon." A glance at Clark. My voice lost in the noise: "check in." His smile told me he didn't hear me but understood. A glance at Matt. My lungs against the world: "check out." In–out. The three of us flew.

I didn't enjoy that first jump much. All of me was focused on watching the instructors and following instructions, checking the altimeter, meticulously recalling what I'd learned the day before. I can only say I had an enormous urge to be on the ground.

I won't dwell on that jump. It went well. I felt great. Forty minutes later, I jumped again—this time with Matt, with Bronte replacing Clark. I enjoyed this one a bit more. I was in my element. My confidence was growing. The landings had been good. I trusted them—and, finally, myself.

Explaining the process of how someone packed the parachutes or the experiences of the others doesn't seem worth it. Everyone did pretty well. End of story.

And then came the third jump of the day. Bronte and Matt again, same sequence. Jack again, paired with Bill and Bronte's husband.

This was meant to be the second-to-last jump of the day. One more was scheduled after lunch. That was the plan.

Back at the door of the plane, at 15,000 feet—my miserable 78 kilos in the air, majesty all around me.

Sixty seconds in free-fall. The cacophony in the instant of my fall didn't merely explode around me; it was an incestuous perception, distorted by a majesty that led to incomprehension, invading my senses and forming a surreal, metaphysical body. A delicate left hand descended softly upon the infinite keys of a white piano, opening a portal into the void. After the heavy descent of the right hand on the row of ivory and ebony, a terrified chimera was released, merging with the wind. A third and final caress on the keyboard sealed the portal. The resonance of the three sounds reverberated in my eardrums, until the spectral silence of its intangible wings settled in—a prelude to what would slowly ignite everything, to what would materialize in my ears and mind. The pianist lifted her gaze from the path of notes, her porcelain cheekbones angled towards the scene. Slowly, the tip of her tongue brushed her upper lip; her head nonchalantly turned, and her hands gave hope to the mythical beast.

There was no cage.

Its breath was the rhapsody for this chaos.

The arc of my body tore through the intimacy of the sky, gravity pulling me down with desperation, while the fragile air offered only minimal resistance, like the joy of someone who neither understands nor wants to understand life. To my left, just behind the altimeter on my wrist, I caught Bronte's smile, gliding at the same speed as mine—her expression, a natural mask of pure confidence built from thousands of jumps, muscle memory, and a sequence as effortless as breathing. I insolently tried to smile back. The altimeter spat out 5500 feet in my face:

Wave!

Reach!

Touch!

Throw!

As soon as my hand pulled the hand-deploy, I saw Matt slip past me on the left, a blur forming a perfect vertical line—like a hand violently tearing a photo, separating us forever. Droplets of moisture burst from my face, and in a matter of six steps, I was jerked to a halt by the deployment of my parachute. My head tilted up, and I felt the tension of the wind filling the canopy tugging at my groin. There was no trace of them around me.

"At what fucking speed were they travelling?" I thought.

I remember the first thing I did was check the bottom skin of the canopy; my eyes, green since I opened them, were filled with a viscous adrenaline—that same adrenaline that sharpened my mind's processes. I quickly assessed: size, shape, slider down, straight flight, and my greatest fear—twist-free. No malfunctions, everything was perfect! I took a deep breath, and as I completed the two flares to ensure the quality of my descent, I thought about how I'd say to Glen in my most nasal voice, "Beautiful jump, mate." How foolish I felt, but it was necessary for the jump to feel perfect. Without a line like that, it would never be a jump worth remembering.

For a moment, the silence in my subconscious cloaked the dramatic trail left by the chimera. It seemed to have vanished, yet this only heightened the sombre, solemn atmosphere that deeply moved me. I closed my eyes for a split second, and when I opened them, the brightness of the world condensed into a single point. Effortlessly, I saw her fingers hover seductively over the keyboard without touching it—a perfect calm, the threshold. Reality ceased to exist; everything was relative.

I wasn't prepared for what happened next. The mythological hybrid reassembled among the galloping particles of the wind, and like thunder, it plunged into the pianist's body. The weight of it bowed her delicate head slightly, her long hair grazing the keyboard as her possessed fingers struck the keys. The sequence of broken chords and arpeggios emitted a fragrance that soothed my inner psyche. From her nails, the furious animal escaped, leaving her under its spell.

The beauty of the world from 4000 feet depressed me heavily; I simply wasn't used to it. It's glorious, seeing the immensity of nature, the endless ocean merging with the sky at the horizon, forming a blue so clandestine and nostalgic that it filled me with power—fleeting power, a single moment, something outside the ordinary, the finest drug. My eyelashes brushed gently against the landscape, savoring the pleasure of squinting as the sun seductively tried to caress them. My fresh breath carried relief, the deepest darkness in my pupils against the vastness of reality, life for a fleeting and shimmering instant had won the fight. There were no clouds today.

The absence of the soft, cloud-like white fabric made the sound waves more perceptible to my collective unconscious. They were waves released from the hammer's strike, layered with wool felt, resonating in the spruce soundboard—waves that had traveled from the mind of the last romantic to his enormous hands on a melancholic day more than 100 years ago. These waves transformed into ink, ink that, as read by countless people, propagated the same waves through time and space: endless oscillations from the headphones of a woman in the rain, her leather boots splashing in a puddle, creating concentric ripples that, from where I floated, resembled waves licking the ocean's expanse.

The possessed woman's right hand grew more expressive, while her left continued playing with chords that added depth and texture to the sound. She tilted her lowered head slightly, looked at me, penetrating, invading, caging me within her hazel irises and her long eyelashes.

A compressed, metallic voice shook me. The radio crackled with my first instruction: "Give me a flare if you can hear me," and I did so without hesitation. "Good job, mate, now head south." Dutifully, I pulled the right toggle, turning ninety degrees to head south—*how obedient I was.* But I trusted that voice, and my instincts told me it was right. "Keep going south," the voice commanded. Yet something in my mind shrieked that I shouldn't keep heading south, that I should turn right again, ninety degrees, to get back to a safer spot. But without questioning it, I followed what the voice dictated. "Turn ninety degrees west." I checked my altimeter—I was close to 1000 feet above a point that wasn't my holding area. Panic rose in my chest, but I clung to the idea that the voice couldn't be wrong—600 feet. "Very good, Jack," the fucking radio declared. A thousand curses leapt from my mouth like water spilling onto hot oil. I was heading downwind straight for the bush. There was no way to avoid crashing through the branches that seemed deceptively far away. I was surrounded—left or right made no difference. I had been following Jack's instructions. I wasn't Jack, and in that moment, a brutal realisation hit me: in a few minutes, I wouldn't be myself anymore—damn it. My entire body tensed, and I could almost see La Parca filming me with a camera, capturing the tragedy, zooming in on my panic-stricken face, the parachute speeding towards the ground faster every second, the wind rustling the heavy branches. This time, the trees didn't speak to me. Why… Life changes in two minutes.

Trapped with no way out, my mind searched in the void for a way to prevent the impending event. My eyes saw only the yellowish green beneath my feet, and the complicit wind dragged me faster and faster. Without asking, I felt the beast's roar in my ears. I couldn't see her or her progenitor, but the breeze rushed with increasingly ornate tones from her right hand, while her left hand maintained the dark, steady rhythm. The right absolved me, and the left condemned me. I wasn't in the world; I was in the melody. Each blink created a new setting, each sound shattered the uncertainty. The harmony modulated, breaking the darkness of C-sharp minor, generating, deep within my soul, a strange sensation of movement and progression.

My mind drained the colour from the world; everything turned to black and white, as if my reality demanded drama. My altimeter read 300 feet.

There would be no diagnosis of an incurable disease in the prime of my life, no old age spent in solitude, bidding farewell to the world in a somber, distinguished hospital, no violent robbery leaving me bleeding in the street. My head wouldn't hang out of a bathtub in a hotel room, surrounded by lines of cocaine, with blood dripping from my nose, showcasing my recklessness, Depeche Mode in the background—that too was ruled out. I would not die of love, or of the absence of it...there were no yellow butterflies around me. This moment was so powerful it obliterated all the possible ways I might have left the world. The last song I had listened to was "Zun Da Da" by Zion— those violins sending *chaos* to the eternity, what a pitiful and ironic choice. The last author I had read was Clarice Lispector—a fitting farewell to the vices of my existence. Terror gripped me when the whispers of my mother's cries and her silent tears streamed across her delicate face in my mind. My pupils held the image, the most unforgivable act: running away from this world before her—"la cagué." I had failed her. There would be no book either. Mierda.

The possessed woman and her beast appeared again. In that moment, they were not two separate entities; the music had fused them into one. Desperation and passion—a creation of urgency and anticipation. It was not my subconscious perceiving this masterful show; it was my inconsolable soul, consuming each movement, each spasm, each sound that was fleeting yet eternal in the wind. Her left claw produced constant, dominant chords, while her right hand wove a melody in a tone more dramatic and expressive. Each melodic phrase expanded and deepened simultaneously in the depths of my being and in the riot of the stars. Tension and instability. Her fingers traced my jaw, calling me enticingly to accept.

Why? Everything was about to end; I knew it. Would I be walking again? Maybe—but I doubted it. I was falling too fast. A branch would tear through my bladder, my legs would snap and get trapped in the undergrowth, my ribs shattered, my spine broken into pieces, my right clavicle would be dislocated, bearing the weight of my fractured neck. Agony, pain, and the incapacity to do anything after being slammed into by nature—that's what I imagined. I would not survive my own life.

The universe abruptly collapsed into a single scene. I swallowed, heard the explosion, and my soul—fully absorbed—watched the whirlwind of fingers mercilessly striking the piano—acceleration and urgency. The music pulsed lustfully around me at an accelerating pace, yet my focus was on the fusion of the two entities. I could clearly see the strain in the muscles of her arms as her ligaments contracted and stretched, veins and arteries pumping venom to the rhythm of her robust heart's beat. Her pupils rose with a delicious slowness, as if climaxing in silence, before vanishing beneath the velvet fall of her lashes. In an unmissable movement, electricity rippled up her spine, the muscles in her back pulled her head upward, leaving her gazing at the sky without the thunderous march of her fingers missing a beat—her nose tilted towards the universe, her eyes rolling beneath her eyelids. In a tension that started from the skin on her hands, she opened her eyes; she hadn't created the music—the music had created her. Her head turned suddenly, tossing her hair aside, revealing her neck—fragile and delicate, provocative. I wanted to smell it, to caress it, to kiss it. Her face filled with life, her lips relaxed and parted, releasing a faint smile, a restrained sigh. That gesture burned the ozone; fire surrounded me. I felt what the mythical Baron de Charlus felt when he saw his beloved Morel playing the violin. The melody in her right hand was desperate, piercing—a scream from the chimera struggling to free itself amid the tension of the low chords crafted by her left hand. It succeeded; the beast broke free and approached me, looking me straight in the eyes.

I was just twenty metres from crashing, mere seconds away from the final act, but my life didn't flash before my eyes. I made one decision: I wouldn't close my eyes. The world's tension wouldn't make me blink. I would endure it. I had to endure it. I might go, but I wouldn't yield—I would stare the great mystery in the face.   No one would know. Falling towards my inevitable fate, I smiled at the chimera, with a look that, alongside the accompanying smile, conveyed a single thought: with pleasure, if I survive, Rachmaninoff will see that, even without knowing how to play a fucking piano, I'll give more life to his music than endless lines of prodigies who only repeated his

Frankenstein. The pianist faded into nothingness, the chords grew less dense, the music more contemplative, three chimes closed the ouroboros—melancholy and resignation. My legs cut through the first branches effortlessly; a blunt blow to my forehead shattered the forest's silence—KO. Trees embracing my skin. My soul breathed. Silence swallowed me. Out of nowhere, I left, and to it, I returned—the fate of us all, to become part of everything, from nothing, once again… there were no angels dancing for me when my fingers spread among the stars.

In a news article written by someone named Josh, the following report appeared:

"A skydiver is safe and uninjured after a dramatic rescue operation on the South Coast of New South Wales, where he became entangled high in a gum tree following a jump near M- Airport.

The man was left suspended upside down at an estimated height of 40 metres, his parachute canopy caught in the upper branches of the towering tree. Emergency services—including NSW Police, Ambulance, Fire and Rescue, the Rural Fire Service, and the State Emergency Service (SES)—were quickly mobilised to the scene.

Before rescue teams could reach him, however, the skydiver performed an extremely risky self-rescue manoeuvre. While hanging inverted, he managed to untangle himself mid-air and shift his weight towards the trunk of the tree. Using the fork of a large branch as leverage, he anchored his parachute container securely, stabilising himself in a sitting position—likely preventing further danger.

A local arborist was later brought in by the skydiving company to climb the massive tree and assist in the technical rescue. Once in position above the skydiver, the arborist rigged ropes, allowing firefighters to lower him safely to the ground.

The full operation took approximately two and a half hours.

Remarkably, the skydiver walked away from the harrowing experience without injury."

What I believed to be the fingers of my right hand spreading among the stars in the dark curtain of the universe, in the void, was actually daylight filtering through the branches and leaves. It flickered as if I had been asleep for a long time and wasn't accustomed to the brightness of the world. I closed my eyes, took a breath, and thought, "sweet fucking baby Jesus—jueputa, estoy vivo". I didn't thank anyone for the miracle. Not God, not gravity, not the gum tree. I should have. I will. I had literally *"entré a la nada y de la nada escapé y irónicamente nada me pasó."*

I felt my left leg strangled by branches and water on my right arm. I could see a small crack in the plastic of the goggles I was wearing. I was hanging by my legs and my left arm. Pain hadn't arrived yet—only discomfort, like my body hadn't realised the story it had just survived.

The heat felt hellish, my temples were screaming for relief, but my right arm, not governed by discomfort, reached up and removed the radio from the helmet. I watched my hand trembling as it held the device. I put the antenna close to my mouth and began turning the channel selector knob. The damn radio I had was supposed to be on channel six—no surprise, it was already on channel four. I was afraid the radio would slip from my hand. I felt utterly exhausted. There was no panic yet.

I pressed the PTT button. One second.

"Hey, I need help—I'm stuck in a tree."

I released the button.

A second later, Bill's calm but assertive voice came through:

"Victor, are you okay? Do you have any major injuries or feel any broken bones? We're on our way to where you are now."

He didn't say it exactly like that, but that was basically the information he gave me. It was my turn to reply.

"Yeah, I'm okay, but I'm immobilised. My legs are trapped and one of my arms is in a weird position."

I couldn't even describe how I was utterly *embarrassing*.

Bill answered, "Don't worry, we'll be there shortly."

I was at the mercy of nature. The wind blew playfully, rocking me like a mother lulling her beloved baby—or pushing the branches with murderous intent.

Not even Solitude was with me in that moment. Apparently, it was waiting for me in the beyond of the beyond—I had stood her up.

How ironic.

I felt so defenseless. Lucky, and at the same time not quite. Why didn't this happen to one of my other teammates, the ones who seemed more clumsy? But then my mind constructed a defensive barrier: it didn't happen to them because they probably would've died—but not you, because...

At least my sense of superiority was still with me, and the bitch only grew stronger in the midst of uncertainty.

The scent of sun-warmed eucalyptus was already making me dizzy, and the sounds in the bush grew more and more encapsulated in silence—one of those silences where your breathing becomes part of it. I even thought about trying to sleep—stupid as it sounds—because I felt I was tangled in such a way that the very mess I was in might be the thing saving me from falling.

Suddenly, the radio crackled to life. Its sound waves shook loose the dust already clogging my pores, dust that would soon turn to mud once fused with my sweat. It was Bill. His calm voice told me he was already there, beneath me: "Don't move. The position you're in looks stable. More people will come and we'll get you out."

In that moment, fear consumed me. It swallowed me whole—didn't even chew. How the fuck was he under me and still needed the radio to talk to me? Worse yet, if he really was below me, why couldn't I hear him? Was he lying? Or at what ungodly height was I hanging? I couldn't look down—only up. Way up. The frustration of not knowing how far I was from the ground gnawed at me.

I grabbed the radio and pressed the button: "Bill, how high am I?" Silence. Then: "Pretty damn high, mate."

Why? Why? God, why? My mind screamed. Silence. Bill again: "Don't try anything. Don't move. The branches are holding your weight. Everything's gonna be all right. The position looks awkward but we'll get you out. It'll be fine."

I took a breath and decided to trust Bill's voice on the radio—but it wasn't enough. I was too uncomfortable. Fear had already swallowed me and now its stomach acid was burning through my sanity.

My right arm was free. Exhausted, but my instincts whispered sweetly: *Save yourself, motherfucker.*

First move: I placed the radio antenna in my mouth and threw my right arm towards where my left was pinned. It felt like the tree had a black belt in jiu-jitsu and had me in an arm-bar. I lifted a branch slightly with my hand without letting go, and pulled with my shoulder—freeing the arm. My weight now hung entirely from my legs. Immediately, my left hand gripped the same branch that had trapped it.

Bill's voice—no longer the cool Bill—yelled through the radio: "What the hell are you doing?! Don't move!!" I would've loved to respond, but my arms were too busy.

Sorry, Bill—I can't answer you now.

Twenty seconds later, I took a breath and, like a snake, wrapped my right arm around another branch. Then I yanked at my right leg. The fabric of my pants had tangled with a seductively curved branch. Why me, damn it? I pulled hard. The damn cloth was top quality—tough as hell—but the wild creature inside me had no limits. The branch snapped, and my leg came free.

This time, Bill didn't speak through the radio. He screamed—his voice broke the silence of the bush: "Don't move, damn it! You're going to fall!!!" I took it as a challenge. With my right leg now free, I swung it onto a branch like a spider monkey's tail. My idea was to pull my left leg next—it was caught between two branches. It was more about rotating the ankle and sliding a bit. That's what I did. I felt pressure that seemed ready to snap my tibia and fibula if I pulled wrong, but ironically, luck was on my side—like it always has been—and I pulled. A delicate move. I felt the branch tearing my fabric, scratching skin. Pain—and a lovely scar.

I was free. I could finally see the ground. Bill really was beneath me—he looked microscopic. I was very, very high. Luck wasn't so much on my side, after all.

Bill: "Victor, don't move any more!!" Once again, it sounded like a dare.

Bill had started off as the Emperor Marcus Aurelius of the skies, but ended up as a Jesse Pinkman in an instructor's jumpsuit—his calm Stoic composure cracking under the pressure of my reckless defiance.

Years of physical training, body work, and constant fights with reality had created a body designed for that moment.

I positioned my arms on two branches. I had my back turned to the world—the same world that had turned its back on me so many times. Without knowing gymnastics, I leaned all my weight on my arms, tightened my core with everything in me so my legs wouldn't fall heavy. My triceps were burning—on the verge of incineration—as I pushed my body up. The branches shook, but didn't break.

I was now sitting between two branches. My heart was pounding—felt like it would burst, if it hadn't already.

From that position, I started to crawl backwards towards the trunk. I still had the parachute pack on. As soon as I reached the base of the branches near the trunk, I wedged the parachute between two limbs like a fork. I could finally rest. I was in a slightly less uncomfortable position, nearly seated. My whole world bathed in orange light. I couldn't hold the radio in my mouth any longer—it fell. I fainted for a few seconds.

I had become a victim of "orthostatic shock while suspended"—the very harness that had saved me was now compressing the main arteries and veins in my legs, cutting off venous return to the heart. The heart that hadn't escaped. The heart that still belonged to my ex-enemiga. For some reason, when Bill's voice pierced the veil of my consciousness again, she was the only thing in my head.

But I won't go into that yet.

"Don't move, Victor, please."

Poor Bill. I gave him more tension than his 3,000+ skydives ever had. With my free hand, I threw up the sign of the horns (malocchio). He probably hated me in that moment.

Soon, I saw people in yellow in the distance. Then green. Then blue. They were either coming to watch the show or to save me. Among them, I saw Bronte and Matt.

They shouted things to encourage me. Horns up for everyone! I was too exhausted. I was a fucking rockstar. It had been two hours.

Bronte's husband (a professional arborist) climbed a tree parallel to mine. He was absurdly agile, focused—like he had done this in another life. From his position, he built an improvised system using a thick branch as an anchor point. I watched him from where I was still suspended, trapped in the vertigo of height, as he tossed me a rope. At the end of it, dangling, was a metallic carabiner, spinning slowly in the air like a coin tossed to fate.

I caught it—my arms still trembling—and without saying a word, clipped it to the parachute harness across my chest, where the weight of the scare still sat. The system was simple, but at that moment, it felt like choreography between branches, friction, gravity, and trust. They used the branch as a pulley, and from above, they began lowering me—slowly, deliberately, as if not to wake Death, who dozed beneath the ground.

I felt my body descending, dangling by a thread—thin, but absolute. The branches brushed against me—some soft, others like inquisitive fingers. I slid past bark. The sun burned my face. My sweat had become part of my skin. The wind blew with ceremonial silence.

That's how I descended—without saying a word—until my sneakers, still stained with dried blood, kissed the earth.

It wasn't heroic. But it was a quiet return from the other side.

Everyone applauded.

Physically, I thanked those men and everyone around me.

Mentally, I thanked God—and my mother, who every night, wrapped in her Catholic-Christian faith, prays for me. In her bed, before closing her eyes, she repeats in her mind—followed by the whisper of her voice—an Our Father, a Hail Mary, her personal petitions, and Psalm 91, where she pleads for my well-being.

Her prayers were interwoven with the countless promises and thoughts I had at the top of the tree.

Time and space: non-existent between us.

1 He that dwelleth in the secret place of the most High shall abide under the shadow of the Almighty.

I'm going to walk away from this—I can feel it in my bones. Just give me one chance, and I swear I won't waste it.

2 I will say of the Lord, He is my refuge and my fortress: my God; in him will I trust.

Mamá, I won't leave before you. I can't go before you.

3 Surely he shall deliver thee from the snare of the fowler, and from the noisome pestilence.

I had to finish the fucking book—but now it wouldn't be one book; it would be many. I'd balance my position in capitalism through art.

4 He shall cover thee with his feathers, and under his wings shalt thou trust: his truth shall be thy shield and buckler.

I remembered Hemingway's words. Why?

5 Thou shalt not be afraid for the terror by night; nor for the arrow that flieth by day;

"I believe that basically you write for two people: yourself—to try to make it absolutely perfect. Then you write for who you love—whether she can read or write or not, whether she is alive or dead."

6 Nor for the pestilence that walketh in darkness; nor for the destruction that wasteth at noonday.

The fairest of the fair—your brown eyes, your voice that lights up my everything.

The photos of you and me, me and you, lying across my books—lifeless, nearly dead—receive life from the love I give them.

7 A thousand shall fall at thy side, and ten thousand at thy right hand; but it shall not come nigh thee.

The world I still had to travel. All I had yet to survive.

8 Only with thine eyes shalt thou behold and see the reward of the wicked.

My father—the most intelligent man I've ever known, even if we don't have the best relationship.

9 Because thou hast made the Lord, which is my refuge, even the most High, thy habitation;

My friends, who are like brothers to me.

10 There shall no evil befall thee, neither shall any plague come nigh thy dwelling.

My grandparents, watching from heaven, smiled gently—realising the wind hadn't yet carried my embrace back to them.

11 For he shall give his angels charge over thee, to keep thee in all thy ways.

For the pain that forged who I was, who I am, and who I'll become.

12 They shall bear thee up in their hands, lest thou dash thy foot against a stone.

For my mind—that challenges me, saves me, and makes me stumble.

13 Thou shalt tread upon the lion and adder: the young lion and the dragon shalt thou trample under feet.

For my body—that saved me today and came out unharmed.

14 Because he hath set his love upon me, therefore will I deliver him: I will set him on high, because he hath known my name.

For Proust, a master I never met.

15 He shall call upon me, and I will answer him: I will be with him in trouble; I will deliver him, and honour him.

For the blessing of being able to breathe—and say that once, I was truly happy.

16 With long life will I satisfy him, and shew him my salvation.

For God the Father, who showed me He is present in all places.

Thank you, Lord.

As soon as my feet touched the ground, two paramedics came up to me, offering their shoulders and asking if I could walk. My head was still spinning from what had just happened. I told them I felt fine. I was thirsty but didn't say so. I could feel people surrounding me and all I wanted was to be alone. My hands, no longer trembling, removed the harness. A police officer asked me for some details while the paramedics looked at me, smiling, asking if I wanted to go in the ambulance to the hospital for a check-up. I declined. I was fine. I had a blow to my right elbow that hurt like hell and a cut on my left leg that didn't need stitches. I was fine—literally. And as cliché as it sounds, I had more life in me than when I jumped from the plane.

All the firefighters, paramedics, police, and other rescue team members—or whichever agency they belonged to— began to leave. The show was over. There was no tragedy, only a story to tell. When Bronte's husband descended, I shook his hand and looked him in the eyes. I said slowly and with intention: "Thank you so much." He casually replied, "No worries, koala—you just owe me a case of beer." I know he was joking, which is why, when I had the chance, I gave him two.

Bill looked at me, and I could tell I wasn't his favorite person—but he was glad nothing had happened to me. He confirmed it with a tone that was sincere, but emotionless. Seneca had repossessed his emotions.

We walked a bit. They had brought down my parachute and tossed it into the back of the truck Bill had arrived in. I got into the back seat with the hero who rescued me and with Matt. Bronte was in the front. As soon as the key turned in the ignition, the radio came on, and in my ears, Mac Miller's nasal yet warm voice began a journey through my nervous system, which was still on high alert.

Follow your…

His gutterspine language kept flowing, leaving behind a catchy melody stuck in my head. There was joy and optimism buried among the countless stupid things the song said. Stupid things I'd already memorised.

Espejito, espejito… I didn't need to ask. Of course it was me.

As soon as we arrived at the drop zone and my teammates—who thought they'd never see me again—saw me, I could sense they were somewhat happy to see I was okay. I didn't think too much of it. I told them briefly that I was fine.

"Follow your drea.." kept playing in my head. That vibrant, festive rhythm wouldn't let me go. Follow your…

I had a brief meeting with the staff and the owner of the drop zone, where they asked me if I wanted to go to the hospital to get checked out. I declined again. More importantly, they asked if I wanted to continue the course. Obviously, I said yes—of course I'd continue. They told me to reconsider, and with nonchalance, I told them everything was fine.

Later, I was able to go to the bathroom—and I was completely dehydrated. When I finally managed to urinate, the scent rose like a ghost off the porcelain. That acrid, powerful stench of concentrated male piss—the kind that strikes the air with such authority that it could have sent Bataille's heroine into erotic delirium—wrapped itself around the cramped toilet cubicle. The yellowish liquid exited my body like a confession, and I took it as a sign that

I needed to drink water fast. I stripped down and turned on the cold shower. I was filthy. My body was battered. The water ran down my mouth, and I drank it with gluttony.

It was 1:35 p.m. I had a burger and a Red Bull for lunch, but I wasn't very hungry. I retreated into my phone and headphones, naturally playing that Mac Miller song over and over again.

At 3:00 p.m., there would be more jumps. Out of courtesy, they asked if I wanted to jump again, but advised me to leave it for the next day.

By 3:57 p.m., I had landed without a single issue after an almost flawless jump. My arm was badly bruised. I'm sure I don't have any fractures, but the swelling is getting worse by the hour. There's a small scrape over one of my elbow tattoos, where the flesh—because of the swelling— looks like it's about to burst. But follow your dre...

And here I am. It's 1 a.m., and I'm still writing—still recounting what happened today. I haven't told anyone. I was tempted, but I don't think it's the moment. I need to sleep because in a few hours, there'll be more jumps. I need to rest and follow my dreams.

Sunday, 20 October, 5:37 p.m.

I just finished unpacking, half-organising, and trying to wash all my dirty clothes in one load, hoping that the eight dollars I have in coins will be enough to get it all dried in two rounds of the dryer—four dollars for 45 minutes, damn system! I'd hate to have to go out again just to get more coins.

As the reader (if there is a reader) might assume by now, I'm back home, which means I survived the skydiving course—complete and happy with the experience, though still licence-less (cue pre-recorded laughter in the background). Despite my attempt to keep jumping, the raffish swelling in my elbow that had spread down my arm couldn't be hidden, even though I tried wearing a hoodie under the 27-degree heat. It was written in the ninth jump—discomfort during flares and holding stable positions was anything but inconspicuous.

Bill, with stoic seriousness, read the situation masterfully. He didn't focus on my arm but instead laid things out in a way that would lead me to choose to postpone the course. With his calm tone, pronouncing each word with perfect cadence and never using a single word more than necessary—if he were a writer, he'd have better economy of language than Flaubert. The bastard had such a controlled aesthetic density that it was hard not to admire.

He told me bluntly that it would be very difficult for me to get the licence, since I'd need at least 10 accurate landings within a 30-metre radius of the designated target. I responded with controlled surprise and refined syntax:

"But Bill, I still have five jumps left." He gave a light pat on my elbow. My face betrayed me with a prolix grimace—needlessly verbose in expression, like a sentence that didn't know when to shut up, revealing I couldn't go on.

I was about to say, "Bill, I already survived an accident. How many have you?" But instead, I just looked him in the eyes and said he was right, that I'd come back once I was recovered—next year. And just like that, my course ended.

One ironic highlight: one of the guys, who sang at weddings, landed on his hand during his fifth jump and broke a finger. You can imagine the look on my face when he told us, with tears barely held back, that he played the guitar at his performances.

Life is both funny and cruel. Not long after, one of my friends contacted me to tell me that a former schoolmate, who already had two kids, had died in an accident back in my home country—on the same day I had gotten stuck in that tree. He had just finished playing soccer and, for reasons I didn't dig into, crashed into a light pole and lost his life. He was the same age as me.

I had kept silent for an entire week. Not merely out of vanity, but out of necessity—and a metaphysical temptation. Or so I told myself: that memory requires witnesses in order to exist. So a few hours ago, I posted a reel on Instagram—badly edited fragments of the week that nearly ended me, without placing too much emphasis on the trauma of brushing against the other side. I mocked myself, of course, like every survivor who refuses to seem pathetic, and let Vince Neil's voice scream in the background: hedonistic, off-key, glam rock incarnate. I wasn't seeking comfort—I was giving shape to the abyss through artifice. Even hell, after all, demands a bit of stagecraft. In short, I gave in to the craving for attention—attention from the sixty people who follow me on that cursed platform.

On the other hand, I feel that my being has been filled with ambition. I've written more about my ex-enemiga and our former relationship than Dostoevsky did about human guilt—and what has ended in reality must also end in the text.

As for her... the last thing I heard was that she had started working at a prestigious hotel facing the harbour. I heard it from her own lips, though that was three months ago.

And, well—if she still lives in this writing and in the silent prayers I whisper each night—where I asked God to shield her from all harm—then maybe my almost extinct faith has started to bloom again, like a weed pushing through cracked concrete. Who would've thought.

Comforting or not, all that remains is the thought that past sorrows might one day bloom into paradise—whether in a few years or many. What difference does it make?

It's been several days since my fingers last danced across a keyboard. November begins. These haven't been good days. I survived falling from the sky, but something still left me lying on the ground. Circumstances I won't name here—not yet. Maybe later.

It's 10:37 p.m. My room feels warm. The lavender Air Wick I just plugged in floods the air, softening everything around me. It's comforting. It was a long day at work— uncomfortable, given my current state—but I kept going. There was no other option.

I would have liked to take refuge in a book, but something pulls at me from within, aching for a different kind of distraction. The answer, as always, is music. But not just any music.

I open YouTube and search: Behind the Wheel – Depeche Mode (Live in Milan, 2006) from their Touring the Angel tour. The song is hypnotic on its own, a metallic and dark spell—the one I always choose when walking alone at night, because it paints new purple shades onto the moon, even when the moon isn't there. But this live version… this one is a beast.

It envelops.

It obsesses.

It seduces.

The word SEX glows faintly on my screen. An industrial sound cuts through the crowd's voice. A camera shot from behind the drums: two arms striking in perfect unison. A pulse of blues and greens in dry, tribal rhythm disguised as electronica.

Gahan—shirtless, black jeans, the closest thing to Lucifer on Earth—pacing between shadow and light. What a dangerously sexy man.

The crowd claps in sync with the bass, which squeezes your chest like a slow exorcism.

The ritual begins.

Floating synths pull me into their orbit. High, distant notes shimmer like city lights far away—cold, but never empty.

A cut to Martin, dressed entirely in black, gripping a red guitar. His hand rises slowly. For a second, the word ENJOY flickers on screen.

Then, that voice. Deep. Paternal. Defeated. My lips mirror it:

"My little girl…"

Gahan and Gore in unison. The camera fetishises the sweat on their faces. The pleasure of inverted control. A shot of the late Andy on the keys. Power wrapped in submission. Strength that finds pleasure in surrender. Worship with a touch of I don't care.

Like the lyrics, Gahan offers himself up—an object to be taken. Emotional eroticism with a masochistic edge.

...

Charlus, smiling from his chateau.

Gahan strokes the mic stand like he's daring you—dare to dominate me, if you're brave enough. He wants to be manipulated.

But only by her.

Ruled only by her.

A nocturnal march into the inevitable.

A wave of arms rises with the music. The seducer walks towards the crowd. The song follows him, he gives himself to her. The tone darkens. It becomes nihilistic. He puts himself on sale—today only. The light shines down as Gahan kneels, countless hands reaching for him. A union. A poem of seduction in disguise—synth-pop cloaked in surrender. The music continues. Kisses are thrown into the air.

I would have given everything to be there, trapped inside that video. To be lost in that bargain-bin orgy of eroticism. To stand among the crowd—with her. Not strong, not weak, just hers. Breathing in the sweat of her neck, whispering:

"You're behind the wheel."

The video ends. I'll switch off this screen once I finish writing.

The darkness will follow me to bed—but it's fine. I know everything will be okay.

The sun will shine a little brighter tomorrow."

X

It is in that "tomorrow" that the text ends. His fingers ceased transmitting his world through this format. The emptiness that followed the full stop left me strangely unsettled the first time I read it. I thought he had ended it intentionally, but something in my intuition told me it had been abrupt. Still, in that moment—back then—my desire to uncover the rest of the story began to grow. It became impossible not to crave resolution. I was reading something in the very place where it had been written, my eyes capturing lines on the screen, separated from the moment of their creation by just a few weeks. For some reason, my mind started generating hypotheses about what had happened to this man. His text ended in the first days of November. From what I knew, he had left the house in mid-November. I had moved into this room in early December. We were separated by, at most, three weeks—not even a month.

Looking back now, I realise that as soon as I finished the text, I was far more invested than my past self would have admitted. So invested, in fact, that I began building theories based on the beliefs and knowledge I had at the time—constructing entire worlds that revealed both my deep imagination and my naïveté.

Now, as I sit here—nearly collapsing under the weight of the early morning, taking slow sips of water—I can see the person I used to be. But more than just seeing what he looked like, I see how he thought. How he imagined. How he went to bed without a drop of sleep after dissecting the text—repeating to himself again and again:

"The author, Victor, lied. What happened isn't true. There's no light around him."

Then, as if a flare went off in his grey matter, he sat up. Without turning on the light, he grabbed his phone, opened Google, and typed:

"M- skydiving accident October 2024."

He clicked the first link and read what the USB document had already revealed—the accident was real. It had actually happened. There was no lie in that.

But for my past self, there was no truth in Victor's behaviour toward the woman he loved. A need to turn him into the villain began to grow. It wasn't possible, not for my twenty-year-old mind, that someone could simply say "She left me, and I accepted it," after displaying such obsessive tendencies in his writing.

I didn't believe him.

To me—the person I was—there had to be another reality.

That's why the text stopped dead.

That's why he left the house.

He did something that forced him to go.

I was sure of it.

He, Victor, had woken up after describing the Depeche Mode song. It was 6 a.m., and his alarm was dragging him out of bed. He hadn't slept well the night before—his mind haunted by the recurring thought of getting her back.

My past self started crafting a narrative:

Victor was feeling unwell because, although he didn't say it in the text, his ex had contacted him after hearing about the accident through social media. And seeing a glimmer of light in that gesture, driven by his own weakness and lack of control, he misread it. He mistook her genuine concern for a desire to get back together.

But something she said shattered that illusion and brought him crashing back to earth.

That's why he felt terrible in those early November days.

That's why he stopped writing.

That's why that morning, when he woke up believing the sun might shine a little brighter… he discovered it wouldn't.

The night before, he had sent her a message filled with love and confession.

She, upon reading it, chose not to respond.

Or perhaps she did—perhaps she said she understood, but that she was now happy with someone else, and that they could still be friends.

His shining sun turned grey.

He couldn't accept such a decent reply.

So, as soon as his green eyes absorbed that information, he vomited it back out in a fit of impulsivity—five calls. Maybe six. All unanswered.

On the other side of the line, she stared at her phone in silence, watching it light up again and again with the name of someone who no longer meant anything to her.

It couldn't be any other way. My theory— or rather, the theory of the man I used to be—was controversial: she lived in the obsessive thoughts of the writer, and he was inhabiting mine more than he should. I could imagine Victor, after typing his last line, continuing to write reality—but constantly deleting it out of shame. It wasn't the ending he hoped for, but it was the ending my mind, in the darkness of that room, was constructing.

In his verbose prose, he had written that after she failed to answer his repeated calls, he claimed to have faced reality and moved on. But that wasn't what he was truly writing in real life. That's why he deleted it.

He never wrote about his brilliant idea to go and find her, to confront her. To go to her house, take her by surprise, with lines rehearsed in his head, asking her to reconsider everything. A warm morning, a set of desolate streets, spring green amid furious reds and yellows blooming in the flowers. Dry footsteps on the asphalt, his mind imagining how she would take him in her arms and kiss him after a dramatic "I can't live without you." Each step reinforced his idea, but the shadow he cast on the sunlight ground wanted to run from the embarrassing incident to come.

Of course he knew where she lived—how could he not? He positioned himself diagonally across from her wooden or metallic door, hoping not to be seen immediately, but to be felt on first glance. Knocking would seem desperate. Waiting seemed the better option. But waiting didn't suit him. So, with one press of his index finger, the doorbell rang. An uninvited visit.

The absence of movement inside tormented him. Ringing again would feel urgent. A third attempt would reek of desperation. Who might she live with? He never mentioned that in the text. But it didn't matter—whoever opened the door, the script was already prepared. Or maybe it wasn't.

No one answered. Should he call her and say "I'm outside your house, please come out"? Or better—send a message?

Me, lying in the bed where he used to sleep, saw that same naïve and obsessive ghost reaching for his phone, about to call, when a movement inside the house made him abort the mission.

Who would open the door, he wondered with growing desperation?

Even though I wasn't there, I know it was her. A little confused—classic movie cliché—the door opening slowly, her in sweatpants she used as pyjamas, her hair tied up, head turning slightly back as if letting someone inside know she'd be back shortly after checking who was at the door.

It was too late to retreat. The morning breeze had already stuck to her face. He looked at her, forgetting everything he had planned to say. She said nothing. An unwanted surprise.

I always knew she wouldn't say anything cruel. Just a "What are you doing here?" and him, stumbling, voice cracking, hands trying to explain what his vocal cords couldn't. She, arms crossed, listening—watching this man deform before her eyes, becoming more and more repulsive to her. Pity, and perhaps a bit of disgust.

He, interpreting it as if he were winning her back.

I, in my bed, filling the blank space that begged to be painted in his story.

Silent arguments. She trying to explain something that didn't need explaining. He explaining something irrelevant to her. A voice from inside—probably another woman—calling her. She saying goodbye and asking him not to come back.

He, speechless, confirming with his silence that he would.

The door closing.

He, compelled to ring the bell again.

Why did my young mind want to see him humiliated?

He had probably lived in that house for about fifteen more days before moving out. I, almost a month after his departure, was filling in those same days with my mind and free time. But I needed to give more meaning to my theory. I read the text again. There weren't many clues—only at the end did he mention that his ex worked at a hotel in front of the harbour. At one point in the story, he worked at a fast food place. Not very helpful. My only option was to ask the people living in the house more about him. It might seem suspicious, but I had the perfect excuse: I had found something that belonged to him.

I worked up the courage, but I didn't get much information. "Call the real estate agency, they should have his contact," was the answer I got. No one in that house cared about anyone, and there I was, caring about someone who no longer lived there.

What had happened?

Why had he left the house?

Why didn't he finish the text—or was that the ending?

Was it all just fiction, or had there really been an ex-girlfriend?

Why had he left the USB in that drawer?

Who used a USB in 2024?

The screen lost its light while I was immersed in my speculations—memories not so clear from those days, but I do remember how I used to think. I recall those moments, colourless and muted, more vividly than anything I did last week. I don't want to press another key. I want to let my eyes rest, get up from this warm spot, and go to sleep. I don't know what time it is—knowing would require the screen to light back up. But the time doesn't fill me with urgency; I know it's time to rest, to push my numb body from the chair and deposit it beneath the sheets, close my eyes and plunge into the current of my unconscious.

I tap the screen and it reveals it's 3:35 a.m. It's funny—on previous reads of this text, I always thought of the narrator. Now I think of myself, reading it, creating plots out of what wasn't written—reigning curiosity. Those December nights when I planned to walk around the harbour area, hoping that by some stroke of luck a woman resembling Victor's beloved would stroll in front of me. Me, in a hypnagogic fog, interrupting her walk, suddenly possessed by a confidence I didn't own. Her, not questioning who I was but trusting me— telling me her side of the story. The two of us walking, looking for a place to sit, her voice shifting tones around me:

"I told him not to come back to my house uninvited,"

My face responding with a grimace of distaste, especially when she began telling me that she felt him lurking around every corner, that every vibration on her phone was another pathetic attempt to get her attention.

The silence I gave her was filled in by her voice—inside my head. A barely perceptible leap: a new story. She tells me that one Saturday in November, she had planned to go out with her partner for some drinks. The two of them, in a bar, laughing, in a healthy relationship—colourful cocktails and good snacks.

Meanwhile, the version of me inside my imagination visualises the scene—imagining inside imagination. A cool night, perfect for a walk, a crescent moon with several silver stars flickering and inflaming intimacy. She felt comfortable with her boyfriend, their fingers intertwined, their steps syncing perfectly—two people or perhaps just one entity.

I was an overly intrusive pedestrian following them.

She, feeling festive and eager to have a great night. He, making her feel safe and content. They enter a bar. Gin and tonics. They share their secret story through calculated smiles and glances that transported them into future realms—both imagining themselves in a future imagined by me.

A pause. Her voice lowered, as if afraid of being overheard—but then rose with a mischievous spark. Everything turned into blue and white electricity—perfect build-up for a juicy anecdote:

"I had a feeling,"

I interrupt her with my dry, disgusting voice, trying to sound like a man:

"No way… don't tell me he showed up."

A twisted smirk formed on her face, a mixture of disdain and irony:

"We were leaving the bar around 2 or 3 in the morning…"

I saw her in black, with her partner, stepping out of the bar, and in the unmistakable shadows—him, also dressed in black, staring at them both. A man with a mind full of anxiety and fear.

The beating of three hearts at the same time: hers, his, mine.

Her boyfriend sensed something was off. Before he could ask, she tightened her grip on his hand—that gesture answered everything.

"Of course he asked me if everything was okay," she said.

The intruder never looked away.

She turned her back on him and walked away with her partner.

Inexplicably, a voice called out her name. He looked back. She pulled forward. Both turned around at once.

The dramatic man, seeking answers that no longer existed, tried to get closer. The air filled with fear, unbearable tension.

She told him firmly not to bother her.

He stepped in further, saying he didn't want to cause trouble.

Discomfort in the new man. He interrupted:

"Who the hell are you?"

The intruder responded—aggressively, incoherently.

She dragged her entire world and said, "Let's go."

A confrontation.

The morbid glee on my face, my eyes wide—not in shock but in delight.

My breathing slowed. She could see in my expression that I wasn't worried—only expecting something filthy and inevitable.

She continued the story.

I was part of it now—a spectator of someone else's tragedy.

Shoving.

The deranged man trying to reach her, to convince her.

People around, witnessing the disgrace.

I was among them.

Her pale skin blushing and then paling again as she saw this man couldn't grasp that he was unwanted.

A hint of pity in her voice as she described the dull sound of the impact.

Victor, on the ground, holding his face.

The night's darkness hiding the scarlet wetness.

Dressed in black so no one could see the filth.

Tears in his eyes—not from pain.

Shouts and laughter.

She and her partner walking away.

The world turning its back on him again.

Their faint smiles betraying pity and irony.

No memory of how I said goodbye to her.

Me, walking away from that scene in a hypnopompic haze.

Returning to my bed.

Back to the glow of the computer screen.

My past self was utterly obsessed with giving the story an ending—or better yet, discovering what had truly happened and relishing every detail if it matched, or defied, his assumptions.

Back then, the abrupt end of the text haunted me. I reread it countless times, each time hoping I'd missed a clue. There was something deeper than curiosity or uncertainty—it was the silence.

It felt wrong that no one seemed to know anything. Each person locked in their room, lost in their own mind—living, yes—but with no interest in who shared their bathroom, who might be stealing their toilet paper, or using their toothbrush. No one asked why he'd left, or what had happened. We all lived under the same roof, yet were only thinking about moving on to another house with new ghosts.

That chandelier in my room—maybe it knew. Not just his story, but the stories of many before him, even mine, which wasn't particularly remarkable. But in the end, to the inert things around us, we're all just dim lights flickering briefly before going out. Our stories—good or bad—mean little. Not even to the people who sit across from us at breakfast for many mornings.

I don't remember exactly what pushed me to act, but some small light had been glimmering in the darkness of my nights.

First, I followed it with my thoughts—then, with my body. I didn't act immediately, but in the abundance of time I had, I decided to test what had been simmering in the oubliette of my mind.

I lived close to the harbour, and the only reference I had was that she worked at a hotel somewhere in that area. My presence there, at different hours, wouldn't seem suspicious. And with the vague descriptions I had, I thought maybe—just maybe—I'd witness a scene I hadn't dared imagine: him begging her, mid-morning, the sun glinting off the boats, and me watching from a distance.

I wandered through cafés and restaurants, spending money on coffee—Monday, Tuesday, and the days that followed—always sitting somewhere new, watching from different angles. I needed to blend in. Every evening, I'd swear I wouldn't return the next day. But I always did. I felt something drawing me closer. Frustration only deepened the obsession—it stretched, distorted, and possessed me. I imagined myself approaching her. Her brown eyes meeting mine. A conversation unfolding.

Becoming an "investigator," if it could be called that, gave shape to my monotony.

A week passed, and no one resembling him or her appeared. I could describe the days in detail, but what would be the point? None of it made sense. But then, one Monday, at around 7:50 a.m., right in front of the biggest hotel—just as the summer sun chased away the last of the morning cold—I saw her.

A young woman in red boots. Her hair was a rich black, tinted with a warm brown—like damp soil freshly turned beneath a shaded tree. It was long and slightly windswept. She wore all black, which made her white skin seem almost luminous. I couldn't quite see her lips, but I knew they were red. Slim. Confident. Walking with purpose. A heavy-looking bag over her shoulder, but her pace never faltered. It was her—I was sure.

She was about 50 metres away. The steam rising from my coffee shielded my gaze. I waited a moment, stood from the bench where my courage had been resting—and it vanished within two steps. I saw her enter the hotel. The glass doors closed behind her like jaws.

I felt relief. And then I cursed myself.

I returned home immediately and reread the text again—like a madman. That night, I went to sleep in a kind of euphoria. I knew that Tuesday—just hours away—I'd return at the same time. This time, ready to speak to her. I had my words rehearsed. I would bring them into the real world.

That Tuesday, I woke up later than expected, as if something beyond me was searching for excuses not to go. Anxious thoughts seeped in from every corner, all trying to cover my insecurity. But something else took over me, and without even showering, I left the house to confront what was written in the blank space—the one I was trying to read by holding an invisible paper against the flickering light of a dying candle.

It was around 8 a.m. when I arrived at the spot where I had seen her the day before. I waited for an hour, fuelled by a premonition that she would appear from somewhere. But she didn't.

Again I felt a strange sense of calm, but it was quickly diluted by my decision to come back the next day. There was no way I would let this moment slip away. Even if she wasn't the muse from the text, even if the text had never had a muse, and was just the creation of a lonely mind—what could really happen to me? An awkward moment? A passing embarrassment? No one knew me. I was nobody to her and would remain nobody whether I approached her or not.

Around 9:15 a.m., I decided to move on. There weren't many people around, and from where I sat, only a multi-lane avenue separated me from the hotel.

As I crossed the street at the light, I caught sight—across the opposite corner—of the woman's steps from the day before. They stood out amid my anxiety: steady, deliberate, sure.

My own steps quickened.

My thoughts collapsed in on themselves. The confidence of her walk evaporated my presence, but I had already surrendered my thoughts. I crossed the street—she was just ahead of me, about to turn toward the sloping hotel entrance. My gaze, lowered in shyness, followed the trail her shadow left behind. We were separated by no more than ten metres. She paused in front of the hotel's threshold, pulling out her phone to check something. That opened the window I needed to make my final move.

As if written by Victor himself, she slowly turned her head and noticed me. Her acknowledgment validated my approach.

The breeze pushed me toward her. Her hand moved slowly to tuck a rebellious strand of hair behind her ear. Her figure was now fully exposed to me, standing against the backdrop of the anchored boats, the port, the pull of the tide.

My lacking social skills had to face her lush, inviting lips.

What a perfect face this woman had.

She smiled at me, and I smiled back. I tried to recall the phrases I had carved into my mind, but they were in a language I no longer knew how to speak.

I felt instant attraction. Her eyelids relaxed slightly, letting a mixture of warmth and challenge seep into her gaze. I swallowed—my throat tasting like red wine on a cold night. Something in her invited exploration, desire, sin. She was intensely sexy.

My timid blue eyes captured every microexpression. I was mesmerised.

My mouth finally expelled a greeting, which she returned without rush, her pupils locked onto my face.

The smile that had accompanied her greeting faded into a more serious line.

My prolonged silence began to make her uncomfortable, the tight line of her lips granting her an undeniable power.

I remembered the text, my thoughts, my sleepless nights, my deductions.

My mouth stumbled toward phrases—some clumsy, making her smirk, others making her uneasy. I didn't ask for her name; I didn't give her mine. From a simple "Hi, how are you?" I fumbled into a string of small talk.

She seemed to respond only because my approach had carried a certain boldness.

I couldn't hold back any longer—nor could she.

And suddenly, without warning, without a red curtain or fading lights, my mouth produced four words:

"Do you know Victor?"

Her gestures froze. My blinking quickened uncontrollably.

It was as if time no longer belonged to both of us.

My confidence grew. My posture changed.

My pupils, like arrows, pierced the shimmering reflection in her retinas.

While the world bathed itself in grey tones, I saw her lips tighten just before she swallowed—a painful swallow, as if a freshly unearthed memory thickened in her delicate throat.

She was battling something much bigger than mere nerves.

Her earlier confidence had vanished. Her eyes, now stripped of defiance, looked almost childlike—searching for refuge where no confrontation could reach her.

Her lower lip trembled slightly.

My mind trembled with it.

Her eyelashes seemed to thicken, no longer brushed by the wind—only shaken by the silent quake starting deep within her chest.

I understood. My blinks, my fears, synchronized with hers.

We both saw the terror in each other's eyes—in each other's souls.

The tension was unbearable.

It was accelerating our mutual decay.

In that moment, she saw the man who, twenty years from now, would remember this encounter.

And I saw her, aged, as if the Mediterranean that once sculpted her presence had now dried her under its unforgiving sun.

Her skin, once luminous like the morning over a whitewashed harbour, had turned into the muted hue of a saline afternoon, weathered by time.

Her amber eyes remained, but they carried an ancient sorrow—like forgotten ships that no longer find their coast.

She hadn't lost her beauty; she had simply acquired the weight of things that once felt infinite and, without warning, stopped being so.

In that instant, I saw her more real, more alive—and more unreachable than ever before.

From deep within her, from the very darkness of her being, to the tip of her tongue—which tapped against her palate four times—the words I had been dreading exploded outward, piercing my heart as if it could recognise sound itself:

"He took his own life."

There was no court reporter needed for this.

Whatever she had to do had been cancelled.

She waited for me to say something.

But everything in me had shut down.

I didn't know what to say—still don't.

The tension cracked again with her trembling voice.

"How did you know him?"

Her eyes avoided mine.

Everything I was, and everything I am now, begged me to ask how he'd done it.

But I didn't dare.

Pills? Syringes? Ropes? Blades?

A leap into the void?

Only the void remained.

The Sun Shines a Little Brighter Today

I didn't ask why either—

Even more void.

I didn't ask her name.

She didn't ask for mine.

She insisted:

"Tell me?"

My eyes dodged hers.

I thought about telling her.

But nothing escaped my mouth—

Not about the bed where they had once slept.

Not about the USB I had found.

I almost told her.

But I didn't.

If she didn't know, it had been Victor's choice.

And I had to respect that.

Even if I was wrong.

Even if it killed me.

I doubt she would have believed how—or why—I knew him.

Or her.

Eyes dropped to the ground.

To the sky.

Disbelief.

Silence.

Sadness.

Without a word, I offered her my hand.

She stared, disbelieving.

Her eyes—mirrors.

I'm an idiot. Then. Now.

She didn't take it.

She held my gaze.

Distrust.

Without thinking, I turned my back and walked away.

Her voice didn't follow me.

The harbour, in that moment, seemed to gather more strength.

The sky was filled with blues I had never seen before.

The silver reflections on the water danced mischievously, as beams of sunlight drew long silhouettes stretching toward infinity.

It was barely 10 a.m. when I took a few slow steps, my eyes fixed on the horizon.

I closed my eyes and inhaled deeply.

The Sun Shines a Little Brighter Today

In my mind, I saw someone walking into the penumbra.

My eyes became the stars observing his staggered steps.

He was dressed in black; his boots made a quiet, calm sound—like a distant river.

The darkness slowly swallowed him, even though it was he who moved toward it.

The crescent moon illuminated patches of stone and his back as he tried to escape its light.

I could hear the ocean crashing against the rocks—his breathing slow, fleeting.

I opened my eyes and tasted the salt of the sea.

I closed them again—and when I reopened them, tears blurred my vision.

There was no harbour. No sun. Only the night.

Beneath my feet, no pavement.

Only earth, tufts of grass, scattered stones.

I was inside his gaze.

My pupils were his.

His breathing was mine.

I stepped forward—and then again.

We stepped together.

He looked.

I looked.

Nothing ahead of us.

We kept moving.

The edge came closer.

I felt the same tear that slid from my eye sliding from his.

Fear possessed me, possessed him.

He wouldn't stop.

I couldn't stop him.

The clean air rushed in front of us, brushing against our skin.

A siren's song, a final promise.

There was nowhere else to step.

We blinked.

Her mother's prayers had turned to ash before the fire.

I imagined his skull breaking against the rocks, the waves swallowing his reflection, his lungs filling with water, his final panic, the murmur of an old, indifferent world.

We took the last step together.

Our bodies, now scattered particles in the whole.

A colossal snap—one no one heard.

In that moment, I understood what he had understood before he fell—what his ether had merged into eternally:

"The only thing that levels everything is death."

I closed my tear-soaked eyes.

And when I opened them again, the sun shone a little brighter for me.

What a fucking cliché—a real fucking cliché.

Acknowledgements

To God, who has placed luminous souls along my path.

To those who gave colour to this existence, even if briefly.

To the contradictions that taught me more than any truth ever did.

To the moments I almost lost everything.

And to that damn tree—

the one that broke my fall and saved my life.

And, paraphrasing the great Fosse—

thank you, too, to the darkness,

for knowing exactly when to start shining.